Redeeming Grace

-Hills of Habersham: Tallulah Falls-

Denise Weimer

PublishAmerica
Baltimore

First printing

At the specific preference of the author, PublishAmerica allowed this work to remain exactly as the author intended, verbatim, without editorial input.

ISBN: 1-4241-1509-4
PUBLISHED BY PUBLISHAMERICA, LLLP
www.publishamerica.com
Baltimore

Printed in the United States of America

Prelude

Ultimately, all that remains is a heritage.

People can pass it by without even realizing it. Every autumn droves of leaf-lookers bound for the highlands of Georgia do just that. Well, it's not surprising when there're but a few buildings left, no passenger trains belching black smoke into the bright jewel sky, and the mighty river that was once a roar in the gorge is now just a murmur by the road throughout most of the year. The dam harnessed the power of Tallulah Falls but opened the sieve of the town's lifeblood. Then the fires devoured almost all evidence of the grand hotels and homes. It's been mostly quiet here since. The tourists have forgotten "The Niagara of the South."

But I can't forget. I have only a few faded photos of ladies in tall hats and bustled skirts, on the arms of gentlemen who look somber in their black coats, yet I can close my eyes and hear the music and laughter of a bygone era. I think often, and the folks in these parts still sometimes talk, about a red-haired beauty who could sing like an angel—how she lighted here with a broken voice, and a broken heart, and what happened to her, my great-great-grandma…

Chapter One

North Georgia, late June, 1886

By the time the train pulled out of Cornelia, the dusky haze of an early summer's evening embraced the darkening horizon. A red sun hung about an hour's worth above, promising light and heat for the final leg of their journey north, but not much more.

The stocky, middle-aged man who had just boarded took a seat near them. He adjusted his wire-rimmed spectacles, trying to be inconspicuous in his study. Hoping to avoid conversation, Grace turned her face toward the window. Even in areas where people would not readily recognize her, she was accustomed to her vibrant, red-gold hair drawing stares. She didn't think it was in her now to be sociable. The travel that day from Athens had been tiring. And the pall from Savannah, like a dark cloud, still hung so heavily over her.

Then Aunt Martha shifted on the seat beside her. The guidebook that had nestled in the folds of her skirt slid to the floor. Immediately the man bent to retrieve it, saying, "Permit me." With a smile and a flourish he handed it back.

Aunt Martha unbent enough to thank him, studying him with her sharp eye.

"You are, madam, traveling to Tallulah?"

"We are," she admitted.

"There is much your guidebook will not tell you."

"I am sure." Martha Hampton raised one eyebrow and seemed to consider whether this interloper was worthy of further address.

Not about to lose the opportunity to meet this dignified-looking woman with her silver-streaked brown hair and tailored traveling costume, the man hastened to make his introduction. He was Professor Willard Schmidt of the Sibley Institute in nearby Mt. Airy. His green eyes glowed with pleasure as Grace turned to acknowledge him, but to her vast relief his attentions fastened not on her, as she was accustomed to, but on Aunt Martha, his peer in age. Grace was able to merely listen to their conversation while keeping an eye on the lush hills rolling past. It was not hard to imagine them still populated only with Cherokee Indians and a few rugged settlers, as they had been at the beginning of the century, before the Trail of Tears and the "discovery" of Tallulah by the outside world.

"Is Mt. Airy a large town?" inquired Aunt Martha politely.

"Not by the standards of New York, to be sure," Professor Schmidt replied with a sheepish smile. Martha had disclosed the city from which they hailed. "But it is widely known as a resort town due to its healthy air. There is a sizeable Swiss colony, more than one school, mercantiles, orchards…and Colonel Wilcox just completed a most impressive hotel."

"Ah, to rival those in Tallulah," said Martha.

"Well, even our mountain air pales in comparison to the gorge and its many waterfalls," the professor chuckled. "I find myself returning again and again. I am lucky to have friends in the town. I'm sure you've read that the gorge is over 1,000 feet deep, and in less than a mile, the river descends 500 feet."

"Yes, in a series of about six falls. I look forward to seeing it."

"You will not be disappointed. Hopefully you will feel justified in coming all this way, to our Niagara instead of yours." The gentleman smiled, clearly waiting in hopes of an explanation of their motives for the trip. When none was forthcoming, he proved his breeding by not pressing further. But he did ask, "How was it that you came to hear of Tallulah Falls? Through some book on travel or health resorts, perhaps?"

Aunt Martha hesitated. "I did read up on the destination before we embarked, but my knowledge of its existence goes back to my childhood near Savannah."

"I see!" Professor Schmidt eyed her in surprise, but her rigid back again discouraged his curiosity. Instead he continued, "Yes, planters from the coast built some lovely homes in Clarkesville. And students from The University of Georgia made the trek to the falls long before there was a railroad. Tallulah has had rail service only four years now, but my! What a difference it has already made! Grand hotels with bands playing every night during the summer, all the popular amusements, droves of tourists!"

And he's a veritable tourist guide, thought Grace rather *ungraciously*. She was beginning to be annoyed by their gregarious companion, although she had to admit he was informative. Welcome silence reigned for a few minutes. Grace pondered the soothing effect the sight of the mountains had on her. She hadn't exactly expected to be soothed in Savannah, but she had hoped to find something she was looking for. Some sense of identity, of belonging.

Aunt Martha had not wanted to go. She preferred to remember things as they had been. But Grace had been insistent, and even Martha knew she had no right to deny her niece a glimpse of what might have been her birthright. Their stay in the charming environs of Savannah had been short, though. Martha was unwilling to risk a chance encounter and possible snubbing from any previous acquaintances.

Grace's heart had stirred greatly as they had arrived at what had been Hampton Hall. But an aching loneliness had swept her as she walked the grounds and gazed a long time at the ruins—the brick chimneys that jutted up as a reminder of past grandeur, one fallen, blackened column a reminder of loss. She had tried to envision her mother on the veranda welcoming suitors as Maum Sally had often described, or playing hide-and-seek with Martha in the orchard. She'd listened for the echo of imagined laughter and the whisper of hoopskirts until she knew exactly what Maum Sally would have told her had she still been alive and at Grace's side: "Doan you go lookin' fer no ghosts, Miss Gracie. Not here. You git on wid your own life an' doan spend it pokin' about in de rubble of de past like Miss Marfa."

Trouble was, she wasn't excited about her own life.

"Ladies, we're coming up to the first of several trestles." The voice of the professor broke into Grace's troubled reverie. "This one over Hazel Creek is a triple-decker."

As the engine steamed out over an amazing wooden bridge, Grace's interest was piqued. She leaned forward and gazed down at the creek at least 50 feet below.

"I see why it took so long for the railroad to reach Tallulah," she gasped.

"Yes, it was arduous work, putting it in," he agreed. Then, after a pause, he asked, "At which hotel will you be staying?"

"The Cliff House," she answered without consideration, still looking out her window.

"I thought as much. The owner, Mr. Rufus LaFayette Moss, is quite the man of the town. He is one of our commissioners and quite involved with the railroad. He's raised his family in Athens. Mr. Moss and his wife Elizabeth live at Pine Terrace during the summer months."

"My concern is, does he run a smart hotel?" asked Aunt Martha.

"Oh, yes, ma'am! The finest! It sits on 40 acres and has over 90 rooms. Its dining room seats over 250."

Martha gave something that resembled a sniff. "My guidebook told me that much," she replied. "The Fifth Avenue Hotel is six stories and has 600 rooms and an elevator. I doubt anything in Tallulah can outdo that. But I do hope the food and amusements are at least of acceptable quality."

Uncowed, Professor Schmidt smiled with amazing patience. "Delicious gourmet food, the goods brought in fresh by local farmers. Hiking, lawn tennis, bowling, ping pong, billiards, cards, horse-back and buggy rides. The band in residence is from Athens and renders the finest music for dancing nightly, in exchange for room and board. The hotel is named for The Cliff House Hotel in San Francisco, where the Mosses went on their honeymoon."

10

"Aunt Martha, I'm sure we will be most comfortable," put in Grace. "We aren't seeking grand amusements, anyway, just some quiet and relaxation."

"Relaxation you may find, but The Cliff House is centrally located. It's the heart of the social scene," the professor said. Grace cut a sharp glance at her aunt. Martha must have known this when she made the reservations. Could her aunt not cease to thrust her into the middle of the activity even while on vacation?

Martha ignored her, maintaining her prim reserve. But her next comment and the nervous flutter of her hands betrayed an uncharacteristic fraying around the edges. "I'm just ready to be there. It seems we've been traveling forever."

Willard Schmidt bowed his head in a humble gesture. "If I can be of service in helping you to your hotel, it would be my pleasure," he offered. "The Cliff House is right across the tracks from the depot, but I could collect your baggage and escort you to the desk."

"We would be in your debt," Martha replied, to Grace's surprise. Though considered plain, and a lifelong spinster, Martha had never warmed to any of the few men who had noticed her in recent years. Grace could only guess the gallant attentions of this Georgia resident appealed to her aunt, somehow seeping past the hardened exterior bred by circumstances and life in a northern city.

As they neared the town, one final, impressive wooden trestle would have given a spectacular view down into the gorge. Grace lamented that the quickly descending darkness made only a black, yawning chasm of the scene.

"But you can look forward to the wonder of starting tomorrow by viewing Tempesta Falls from The Cliff House's five-story observation tower," Professor Schmidt told her with a twinkle in his eyes.

It was not too dark, however, to appreciate the beauty of an ornate, two-story building which rode the swell of land just to their left. Lights gleamed beyond the intricate porches, and a cupola crowned the roof. Grace caught a glimpse of a splashing fountain. The professor informed them that this was The Grand View Hotel.

"Why did you not put us there, Aunt Martha?"

The older lady merely lifted a shoulder, reminding Grace that it was not her duty to explain. But she said, "The Cliff House has a well-established reputation, from what I read."

Professor Schmidt had the good manners not to remind the lady of her earlier uncertainties on that score. He nodded. "This is The Grand View's first year in business. Mr. Young will see to it that his hotel is the equal of Mr. Moss'. In fact, you probably would have found The Grand View at capacity, anyway, since Mr. Young engaged Professor Leon to come this next month."

Too tired to ask who Professor Leon was, Grace just assumed he would be conducting some boring botany lecture.

Lights winked welcomingly from the buildings of the town sprinkled on the hill. Everything was concentrated on the south rim of the gorge. The train slowed to a crawl, loudly clanging its bell to herald their late arrival. A bustle of activity exploded on the street as they pulled up to a quaint, two-story wooden depot, painted red with white trim along the windows and corner boards.

"Tallulah Falls!" called the conductor. "End of the line!"

As she stood, Grace peered out the window one more time, seeing what must be their hotel. Two large white structures, looking to be three-and-a-half stories, were connected by two-story porches. Under a striped awning a brass band began to play. The cheerful music made her feel like a visiting dignitary as she stepped off the train.

"Our maid is on the second class car," Aunt Martha told Professor Schmidt.

"One moment then, and I will return," he said.

Grace watched uniformed porters scurry around, loading luggage in wagons marked "The Robinson House" and "The Grand View." She noticed the turntable which would rotate the train to face southwards for the return trip to Clarkesville and Cornelia in the morning. Then Professor Schmidt returned as promised, carrying two valises. Their pink-cheeked Irish maid Maureen followed right behind. A hotel employee had been dispatched with a cart to fetch their larger trunks.

"Ladies, we may proceed to the hotel," said Professor Schmidt. Before following, Grace breathed deeply. It seemed the mountain air, now cool with the damp tang of nighttime, danced right to the bottom of her lungs. She experienced a tingle of promise. Maybe they had been right to come here.

* * *

The first thing Grace became aware of the next morning was the roar of water. It drew her from sleep like a strong current, tugging her eyelids open. She lay in her four-poster bed in her hotel room fronting the grounds.

"I will take the street-side room," Aunt Martha had said in a tone of noble sacrifice the night before. "We did come here expressly for *you* to rest." Implying they would have been hobnobbing at the summer homes of wealthy New Yorkers in Newport otherwise, as Martha had wished.

Her aunt must still be abed. No sound issued from her chamber that joined Grace's by way of Maureen's small sleeping quarters. Above the thunder of the river, there were only a few muted, distant movements of early risers and the chirping of birds. Grace realized that the train commotion and the band music had filled her ears until late yesterday. The initial boisterous tunes had become soothing strains as she laid her head on her pillow.

She stretched and sat up, catching sight of her own reflection in the vanity mirror as she did. Her waist-length hair, the color of russet autumn leaves, was a riotous mess. She had not bothered to braid it before bed. It contrasted with her white cotton nightgown and brought out the luminescence of deep brown eyes and milky skin.

"Youz de spittin' image of your ma," Maum Sally had always said, "'Cept a bit prettier." She had always smirked, as if telling a secret she was only free to share since Louisa Hampton Galveston was long in her grave.

Dear Maum Sally. How welcome her mothering instincts would have been now, at this vulnerable stage in Grace's life. Well, she

13

would have to settle for the cheerful, if empty-headed, bustle of Maureen, the immigrant her father had hired for them when Maum Sally had died.

Grace climbed out of bed. After washing up and changing into her undergarments, she knocked softly at Maureen's door. The young woman's ginger-colored head quickly appeared. "Yes'm?"

"I'm ready to dress." Grace saw with satisfaction that the servant already wore her typical gray frock. She was certainly not lazy.

"Yes, indeed, ma'am," Maureen replied, hastening to the wardrobe and throwing open the door. Inside hung the row of colorful dresses she had unpacked hastily the night before. "And what will it be, a nice promenade dress?"

"I think the violet one."

The costume Maureen withdrew and laid across the bed was all that was fashionable. The violet of the bodice, with its square neck, pointed waist, and *basque*, or tail, behind, contrasted with lavender and aquamarine in the front plastron and the elaborate drapery of the skirt. There was a tall, oval hat to match.

"A very exciting morning, is it not?" bubbled Maureen. "Imagine, we're in *Georgia*!"

As Maureen adjusted the laces of Grace's corset, designed to produce the perfect S-shaped silhouette, Grace pondered all that had brought her here. Really it had been her role as the Messenger of Peace in Wagner's *Rienzi* that had disrupted the flow of her life. Yes, that was decidedly what marked the change. After that she could no longer float along in the anonymity of her life with Aunt Martha and her voice lessons with Monsieur LeMonte. Important people in the world of opera had taken notice of the lovely young soprano, Grace Galveston. Suddenly her name was on everyone's lips. People had begun to predict a major role for her in The Metropolitan Opera's 1886-87 season...the season yet to be. And Aunt Martha was determined enough for it to still happen to take her niece far from the scene of her ambition, and Grace's stress, all the way to the mountains of North Georgia.

Grace struggled into the tight, three-quarter-length sleeves of her bodice and allowed Maureen to work the hooks in back. Then she sat dutifully at the vanity for her hair to be brushed and put up. She only half-listened to the maid's chatter, politely saying "mmm" and "yes" at the proper moments. She was grateful for the maid's ministrations, well aware that like the clothing, this was a luxury bought by her father's money.

But she didn't have to think about that right now. She drew a parasol from the wardrobe and told Maureen, "Please ask my aunt to join me at the gorge overlook when she is ready. I'll wait there for her so we can breakfast together."

"Yes'm." Maureen bobbed a curtsy.

As Grace opened the door, wonderful aromas from the kitchen greeted her. She had to ignore the rumbling reminder from her stomach that she had forgone even her normal morning coffee.

Outside, the grounds of The Cliff House resembled a Monet painting, ladies strolling on the arms of gentlemen in the soft golden light. Grace admired neatly trimmed shrubs, towering trees and colorful flowerbeds as she took the path to the boardwalks that traced the gorge's rim. A bright flash of red caught her eye. She smiled as a pileated woodpecker began a persistent tattoo high up on a nearby tree.

Joining a few others on the boardwalk, Grace wasted no time in looking over. Not much less than 1,000 feet below, the river ran its course, hemmed in by rugged granite cliffs and slopes of hardy oaks and pines. The water was the most amazing turquoise in color. Grace thought the scene looked like a lost paradise.

She was privy to a view of a breath-taking waterfall. A nearby sign reminded her it was Tempesta and was 76 feet high. Alongside the falls, and accessible by catwalks that hugged the cliffs, Grace saw the observation tower Professor Schmidt had mentioned the night before. She gazed a long time at the rush of water between the two pools far below. It truly was beautiful, wild and free in a way that Niagara wasn't, like the red-tailed hawk that launched from some hidden nest on the far rim and soared above the chasm. She liked the sense of power in the wilderness, the reminder of the artifice of modern society. Finding an isolated bench, she sat, closing her eyes, feeling the gentle breeze. She breathed deeply as minutes ticked by unnoticed. Ah, the solitude.

"Surely those people don't intend to *bathe* in that pool!"

The strident voice interrupted Grace's daydreams. She looked up to see her aunt, her opera glasses trained on the scene below. She was clad in a navy walking dress in a style similar to Grace's, including the draped and bustled skirt. Gone were the elegant, dome-like layers of the '70s. The new rage was a shelf-like protrusion to the rear that elicited many jokes about horses and tea trays. But no matter how ridiculous Martha Hampton might have admitted the style was, she would be the last to make waves in the New York City society she so dearly wanted to conquer.

"I have heard that people enjoy swimming in some parts of the river," Grace said.

"But not that part." Martha unfolded a map and jabbed a finger at a section labeled "Hawthorne's Pool."

"Yes, that's it, just above the falls."

Grace peered down at the figures near the mysterious jewel-like pool. The water was sheltered by steep, rugged cliffs on the north rim. "It does look tranquil and inviting."

"The same mistake Rev. Hawthorne made in 1837."

"You knew this Rev. Hawthore?" Grace raised an eyebrow.

"No, no, according to my guidebook," Martha replied impatiently. Grace suppressed a chuckle at her aunt's tendency to gather all the knowledge, and therefore all the control, possible in any situation. "He was from Athens. He preached on a Sunday morning in Clarkesville and then came here with a group of friends. They decided to find a spot to camp. Rev. Hawthorne stayed behind for a swim. Some say all they ever found were his clothes and pocket watch, placed on a pine sapling."

"And does his ghost haunt the gorge?" Grace couldn't resist asking with mock-wide eyes.

Martha smacked at her with a fan, not even cracking a smile. "There you go being pert again."

"Heaven forbid."

"Grace, if you're going to progress during this visit, you really should let go of a bit of that cynicism. No wonder you can't sing with all that bottled up inside."

Grace withdrew into herself, for her aunt's words hit closer to the truth than she wanted to admit. "Perhaps you mistake the intent of my joking. There's nothing wrong with simply having a bit of fun."

"Fun," said Martha, "is laughing, being with other people, dancing, doing things, not going off by one's self or making glib remarks!"

Grace sighed. She did not point out that even though Martha frequently sought out company, she did not often laugh, and she certainly never danced!

"But for now, let's begin with breakfast. A good hearty meal, and then you'll feel up to a hike."

"A hike?"

"Yes, there is much to see. Exercise will put the wind back in your sails. I understand that there is an even larger falls just below this one."

"But surely...you...?"

"Of course not. I'm too old for such strutting about. I'll find a nice companion for you, and I'll see about getting some post cards to send to the right people back home. It wouldn't do for everyone to think we've fallen off the face of the earth."

Martha was already heading back towards the hotel, never having even commented on the view. "It's too bad Blake Greene isn't here to squire you about..." she muttered under her breath.

Blake was the last person Grace would have chosen as a companion right now. Handsome, tall, and intelligent, the Kentucky-born lawyer was both Southern enough and firmly transplanted to New York City enough to win Martha's approval. The money didn't hurt, either. His family raised race-winning thoroughbreds on their farm in the Bluegrass, but Blake had chosen to attend school in New York, thus following in his uncle's footsteps and joining his successful firm. His leisurely courtship of Grace had intensified recently, following the *Rienzi* role that had thrust her into the limelight and the notice of other young bachelors. It was just one more point of confusion in her life. She knew she would have to face it soon, and examine her feelings towards the young man, but she needed this time apart first.

Chapter Two

Their mealtime in the well-appointed dining room of The Cliff House was deemed quite satisfactory, but failed to produce the desired companion for Grace. The ladies spent the morning in town, looking through shops. Around eleven Grace was surprised to spot a soda fountain. A painted sign above the door proclaimed, "Wylie's Refreshments."

"Oh, let's go in," she urged.

At that moment they noticed someone waving to them from a round table near the glass front of the store.

"Why, it's Professor Schmidt," Martha murmured. "...and two ladies." Now it was Martha who sounded surprised.

As they approached, the smiling man rose. He took Martha's hand and bowed over it. "What a pleasure to see you again so soon, Miss Hampton!" he declared with disarming earnestness. "Miss Galveston. I had hoped to be able to introduce you to my friends."

"Oh," said Martha. They both studied the ladies, who had risen as well. One was about Martha's age, the other about Grace's. Both were dressed simply but in flattering outfits. Sincere smiles graced their round faces.

"Mrs. Sarah Wylie, and her daughter, Miss Amelia Wylie."

The young, dark-haired lady added brightly, "And that's my father, Howard Wylie, behind the counter!"

Grace looked to where Amelia indicated. A tall man in a white apron waved to them with one hand while operating the soda fountain with the other.

"You would think he would actually use the help he hires," Sarah laughed. "But nothing makes him happier than tending his customers personally."

"Well, it is a pleasure to meet you," Martha said.

"These are the friends who are kind enough to open their home to me," the professor explained. "And they were most intrigued when I told them of the cultured ladies from New York whom I met on the train. Won't you join us?"

"The strawberry sodas are especially delicious," added Amelia, looking hopeful.

"Just what I had in mind." Grace smiled at her.

The professor pulled out and held the lightweight chairs as the women settled their bustled skirts and drew up to the table. Then he hastened to the counter with their orders.

"My father was just in Atlanta and tried a new drink at Jacob's Pharmacy. They called it Coca-Cola. He thinks it will soon be the craze. Imagine, if the hit drink of the country came out of the South!" The sparkle in Amelia's blue eyes belied the possible sarcasm of her comment. "Of course we know New York is the place *everything* is happening. Have you seen The Statue of Liberty? The Washington Monument? Did you get to see the demonstration of Mr. Bell's telephone?"

Grace laughed and held up a hand. "Yes, sort of, and no," she replied, endeared rather than irritated by Amelia's questions. Even though the girl couldn't be but a year or two younger than Grace was—and she herself had just turned 20—there was an openness, a naiveté, about her that was refreshing. Especially compared to many of New York society and the world of opera, where people often said what they did not mean.

She had read a great deal in the newspapers about the amazing sculpture "Liberty Enlightening the World," given in friendship to The United States by France, and had even driven to the waterfront to view its construction on Bedloe's Island. "The statue is truly amazing, over 300 feet tall," she told her attentive little audience. "It is made of copper sheets on a steel framework. Workers had to reassemble the pieces since it arrived last summer. President Cleveland will dedicate it this fall."

"Oh, how I wish I could be there," sighed Amelia.

"As to The Washington Monument, I have not been to see it at the National Mall, but we did get to view the pyramid when it was on display in New York, at Tiffany's."

"You know it is the largest piece of aluminum in the world, and extremely costly," Aunt Martha added. She looked up as Professor Schmidt returned with their sodas. Ever the paragon of proper etiquette, she explained to him, "We were just discussing the sites and innovations in New York City."

"I see." His eyes lit with interest.

"Tiffany's..." Amelia murmured. She eyed their jewelry and dresses with a new uncertainty. "Do you go there often?"

"Goodness no—"

Aunt Martha cut in. "But you would love to walk the Ladies Mile and see all the grand mansions being built on Fifth Avenue. The marble chateau Alva and Willie Vanderbilt put up next to St. Thomas is the most breath-taking. There are unicorns and sea serpents and cupids on the roof, with copper cresting."

Martha laughed lightly and continued, oblivious to the fact that her listeners were emotionally withdrawing. "People still talk about Mrs. Vanderbilt's masquerade ball of '83, the year they christened their new home. Her sister-in-law Alice came as an electric light, in a white satin gown trimmed with diamonds and a battery-operated headdress, of all things! Can you imagine? Everyone who was anyone was there. I heard that event alone cost $250,000."

"Aunt Martha—"

"And I suppose it did force the old-money Astors to take notice. You wouldn't believe how exclusive Caroline Astor is, she and her social planner Ward McAllister, with their list of 'The Four Hundred.'" Martha sniffed in disdain. "Her annual ball is *the* event of the season. Anyway, they get along now. The Vanderbilts are content since they pressured the opera's board to build The Met. Now there is enough room for all of them, old money and new. What do they call it, where they sit, Grace?"

"Um...the Diamond Horseshoe," Grace replied, her face red. It was clear that her aunt was overwhelming their companions with her lofty talk of the crème-de-la-crème of their city of residence. Martha simply could not believe that everyone would not aspire to such pinnacles of worldly success.

"I must say the Vanderbilts are loyal supporters of the opera, though. I thought Mrs. Vanderbilt's compliments on your performance in *Rienzi* were very gracious."

"You're an opera singer?" asked both the Wylie ladies, almost in unison.

"Well...yes."

"Why did you not tell us?" Sarah turned on Professor Schmidt.

"I—must admit—I did not know," he said, raising his hands in a futile gesture.

Amelia asked in a voice faint with wonder, "Are you a star?"

"I would hardly say so. Lilli Lehmann is the undisputed darling of The Metropolitan Opera."

"Yes, I have heard of her."

"Grace is far too modest," Martha interjected. "She will soon have all the acclaim of Ms. Lehmann and more. People are saying she will receive her first major role this fall. That is, if she can rest up enough this summer to return in full strength of voice."

"Oh, my," murmured Sarah Wylie.

Grace sipped her soda, embarrassed and dismayed. Her aunt's conversation brought memories of the last few months all too unpleasantly to the fore in her mind. Unconsciously her body tensed.

"So, are you here to allow the natural wonders of Tallulah to soothe your spirits?" Professor Schmidt asked. He favored Grace with a gentle smile.

Grateful, she replied, "Very aptly spoken."

Martha leaned forward. "Being thrust into the limelight so

suddenly, among other things, has caused stress on Grace's voice. It is such a delicate instrument, you know. Her doctor and instructor both advised strict rest—a complete change of scenery."

"Oh, well, you've come to the perfect place," said Sarah. "We certainly have the best air and scenery, even mineral springs."

"We enjoyed the view from our hotel grounds down into the gorge this morning. I was telling Grace what a shame it is that I am not robust enough to make the hike to the water's edge. Such exercise would surely do her good."

Sarah opened her eyes wide and turned them upon her daughter, saying with emphasis, "I am sure Amelia would enjoy showing Miss Galveston her favorite trails."

Amelia hesitated, her enthusiasm now subdued by a bit of intimidation. "I—yes—I would be happy to."

"You surely already had plans for the day. I don't want to interfere," Grace said, offering the other girl an escape. But somehow she hoped Amelia would not accept it.

"No, no…it's perfectly fine. I usually just loll about here at Father's store on Saturdays. Going with you would be much more interesting. Where would you like to go?"

Grace shrugged. "You are the local expert. Wherever you suggest."

Amelia told her that Hurricane Falls was the largest at 96 feet, but that the footpaths surrounding it were narrow and treacherous because of the clouds of spray that always enveloped the area. If Grace elected to see it over any number of smaller falls, rapids or pools, she would certainly have chosen the grandest introduction to Tallulah.

"But you'd definitely have to change," Amelia told her. "And wear your sturdiest boots."

Was Amelia trying to test her metal? It didn't seem possible that the sweet young woman would do so out of spite, or to embarrass her. As Grace was thinking this, Amelia's face softened, almost as if she were reading Grace's mind. She added, "We can go very slowly."

Professor Schmidt said, "I think she's hoping to make enough of an impression that you'll be enchanted and stay with us a long time. There's a shortage of young people outside of the tourist season, you know."

"Except for Alice Hargrove," Amelia agreed with a wrinkled nose.

Grace was convinced. She knew all too well about the lack of friends one's own age. Back home, Martha carefully screened all of Grace's potential companions by their social standing. Those who met her requirements were usually found by Grace to be wanting for sincerity.

They agreed to meet at an hour after lunch on the porch of Grace's hotel. Grace was there early. She was just as eager to get out from under Aunt Martha's wing as Martha was to have her go. She gratefully accepted the carved walking stick that Amelia had brought for her use and followed the girl to a trail that descended toward Hurricane Falls. Amelia said she would enjoy taking The Cliff House catwalks to the observation tower another day.

"A lot of famous people have come here," she offered as they brushed past mountain laurel and stepped over tree roots. "Writers, politicians, even General Toombs. He hid in the gorge to get away from the Union soldiers who tried to arrest him after The Late Unpleasantness. Joseph LeConte has come many times to study our geology. But all that probably doesn't interest you."

"On the contrary, I would love to hear anything you wish to tell me. This is all so different for me, I find it fascinating."

Amelia giggled. "Sort of like how I would be in New York City."

She proceeded to point out animals and plants as they hiked. There was everything from a delicate white orchid called "monkey face" to roundleaf sundew, a rare carnivorous plant. Amelia explained that insects got stuck on the red leaves and were thus fated to be nutrients for their captor.

"Yuck," said Grace.

Some ways down the path, a tiny trickle of water made the face of a rock protrusion glisten, and there Amelia stopped. Grace was glad for the break but didn't like to say so. She breathed deeply, enjoying the pungent scent of earth and woods.

24

"See anything strange about this little cliff here?"

"No."

"Look closely." Amelia smiled.

Skeptically Grace leaned in. "Oh!" she exclaimed, for she had spotted a tiny head poking out from a crevice. The water ran right over the pointed nose, which exactly matched the hue of the moss. "The green salamander. Their skin must stay moist if they're to breathe. I like to see how many I can count in one place."

While Amelia did so, Grace studied her companion's face, glowing and pink with the exertion of the walk. It was a simple face, not striking, but it drew the eye just the same. It was clear Amelia was a lover of nature and very knowledgeable about the land that was her home. Despite Amelia's sighing for the big city, Grace could not picture her staying in one for very long.

"Twelve!" exclaimed Amelia with satisfaction. "Well, let's go on."

When they neared the water, the cool mists were refreshing, for the day had grown quite warm. They came to an overlook at the brink of the falls that made Grace quite dizzy. Above, the river seethed and raged like a boiling cauldron. Then, with a roar that was almost deafening, it tumbled through a narrow channel between high cliffs. Below, precarious-looking boardwalks and cables helped visitors descend to the surprisingly calm pool at the base.

"Do you want to go down?" Amelia shouted.

Grace could see that the few people who were bravely struggling to do just that were getting drenched by the clouds of spray. Visions of plunging to her death came to mind. Vigorously she shook her head.

Amelia laughed and pointed away from the falls. "Let's go a ways upstream, then!"

As they beat their way towards the base of Tempesta Falls, it was becoming painfully obvious to Grace that she was unprepared for such rugged terrain. The extent of her exercise in New York had been on the ballroom floor, and that infrequently. While Amelia trudged firmly ahead, she struggled to keep up, leaning heavily on her stick.

Loose gravel rolled beneath her boots, and she frequently had to grab for trees to pull herself along. At one point she incredulously followed Amelia through a crevice in the rocks so narrow that she had to turn sideways.

"We're just threaded the Needle's Eye," Amelia said on the other side. "Some call it Lover's Squeeze."

Grace was panting so hard she couldn't reply. One look at Grace's face caused Amelia to steer her quickly towards a large, flat rock a bit away from the river.

"I'm sorry," she said, uncorking the canteen she had brought along and handing it to Grace. "How thoughtless of me. You seemed to be doing so well, but I should have known—"

"It's all right," Grace gasped.

"We needn't go farther. Let's just rest here a bit." She produced two summer peaches from her skirt pockets and offered one to Grace.

Grace accepted. "I suppose I have a bit too much pride to admit when I'm in over my head." Chuckling, she bit into the firm, juicy fruit.

"It's my fault. But what did you think of the falls?"

"Tremendous. Worth the hike."

"I agree. I always feel God's presence so strongly here. Maybe you do like it well enough to stay a while?"

Grace smiled. "We plan to stay the whole summer."

"Oh, there's lots to do, with all the activities the hotels offer, and there are definitely spots where the water is much more accessible. I'll also have to introduce you to some of the local young people."

"That would be nice. Thank you for wanting to take time with me."

Amelia looked surprised. "Just what I was thinking—about you, I mean. I'm not very exciting company for a high society lady."

Shaking her head, Grace said, "But I'm not—for all my aunt's talk. I'm sorry she went on so at your father's soda shop. She can be a bit—pompous—at times. I was afraid she would completely put all of you off."

"I did find her talk interesting, if a bit—well, intimidating. And I doubt Professor Schmidt could be so easily discouraged. He seems quite intrigued by her. He's rather lonely, you know. I think he leaves his science lab and comes up here in hopes of meeting the right sort of woman."

"Oh!" Grace grew pensive at the notion of the teacher being attracted to her aunt. She had never given much thought to what she would do if Martha ever married. The idea had seemed so unlikely. "Well, maybe he'll find a similar mind in that Professor Leon who's coming to The Grand View, whatever that is about."

"Professor Leon?" Amelia responded with her dark eyebrows winging high above her blue eyes. "Don't you know? I can't believe you haven't heard yet. Professor Leon is not really a professor, he's an aerialist."

"A—what?"

"Yes, an aerialist. His real name is Mr. St. John. Mr. Young saw him walk between two buildings at Five Points in Atlanta and decided that bringing him up here would be just the thing to draw a crowd and make a buck. He's going to walk a rope strung across the gorge later in July."

Grace's mouth dropped open. She shuddered as she imagined such a feat, then the crowd Amelia had mentioned. "This place will be a madhouse," she murmured. So much for peace and quiet.

Amelia nodded and wiped her mouth with her handkerchief, tossing her peach core into the woods. "People are coming from all around. Be glad your hotel room is secured for the summer."

"And I thought I was getting away from all the hooplah."

"Don't you like it? New York City, I mean? Your aunt certainly seems to."

Grace was quiet before she replied, watching the turbulent river. After a couple of men with their shirtsleeves rolled up passed them, exchanging nods, she spoke. "Even my aunt has a love-hate relationship with the place." She laughed a little bitterly. "I think she just wants to show everyone that though she was forced to leave the South, she isn't beaten—that she's as good as they are. She hates depending on Yankee money, but she loves what it can buy. I can't really explain it."

"I take it your mother is deceased?"

"Yes, at my birth. Aunt Martha has been my caregiver ever since." She knew the next question in Amelia's mind, so she headed it off by adding, "My father takes care of us financially but isn't very involved in our lives."

Thankfully, that seemed to satisfy her companion for the moment. Amelia turned her questioning in another direction. "How did you come to be an opera singer?"

"My aunt noticed my voice quite early, of course. When its quality did not dim in my early teens, she convinced my father I needed a tutor. He found Monsieur LeMonte, himself once an opera star." Grace giggled. "The sound of his name spoken with the French accent always used to bring to mind a large citrus fruit. And he *was* rather rotund."

Amelia laughed.

"Eventually he found me parts in the chorus and as an understudy. Then there was a secondary role this past season that drew some acclaim. I'm afraid it all rather went to Aunt Martha's head."

Sighing, she remembered her aunt's triumph when even her father had warmed in his interest, sending her flowers and dresses, and of a finer quality than before. "We'll soon be eating watercress sandwiches and cakes from Dean's in Mrs. Vanderbilt's parlor," Martha had tittered. Grace's father's family had made their fortune with wise investments in mills, a successful newspaper, and railroad ventures. Dr. Hampton Galveston was now, along with his wife and their children, a permanent fixture on Caroline Astor's list of "The Four Hundred."

"It must have been amazing, singing to all those rich and powerful people, all their eyes fixed on you," Amelia mused in a tone of dreamy wonder.

Grace smiled somewhat sadly. "I admit it had its charms. But—" she hesitated, afraid to say too much to this friend she had just met, but who was so easy to talk to, "I never did feel I fit in with them. I'm much more comfortable here."

"Then I'm glad you're here. And I know you're on strict orders not to make a peep while you are, but maybe just once before you leave...I could hear you sing, too?"

"Of course."

Finally Grace felt ready for the return hike to the hotel. She and Amelia parted ways with a promise to play cards on the morrow. When Grace dragged into the elegant lobby, her skirt hem muddy, her clothes dampened from perspiration and the mists of the falls, and her hair straggling down, Martha gasped in horror.

"What in the world happened to you?" she demanded.

"Aunt Martha, what did you *think* I would look like after hiking to Hurricane Falls?" Grace asked her. "Could you please have a tray of food sent up to my room?"

"Well, you're certainly not presentable for the dining room! Merciful heavens!"

As tired as she was, Grace laughed as she climbed the stairs. She had Maureen draw her a warm bath and liberally added scented salts to soothe her aching limbs. Her supper tray arrived as she was toweling off.

While dining on herb-encrusted mountain trout and vegetables, she pondered what Amelia had said about sensing God's presence in nature. She had definitely been aware of a power today, and at the same time, a peace. Even though Maum Sally had sought to teach Grace about a loving Heavenly Father, Grace's experiences since, and even the somewhat stilted church services she had attended, had caused her to believe in a rather impersonal Creator. But maybe there was more to it than she had thought. For she sensed an opening in the heavens as it were, as if Someone benevolent were suddenly smiling down on her.

Grace realized one of the things missing in her life had been a friend. Someone to talk to in an open, unpretentious manner like she had to Amelia today. She *had* been bottling things up inside. She sensed more promise here in little Tallulah Falls than she ever had in New York. Feeling more relaxed than she had in many months, she climbed between lavender-scented sheets. She was asleep the moment her damp head touched the pillow.

Chapter Three

Grace had been at The Cliff House for almost a week when the town celebrated The Fourth of July. She had spent the time reading, playing cards with the elegant tourists with whom her aunt liked to while away the hours, and enjoying ping-pong and tennis with Amelia. Viewing L'Eau d'Or, Oceana, Bridal Veil and Sweet Sixteen falls—and numerous cascades from feeder creeks—had left Grace convinced that each was uniquely beautiful. They had even taken in the waters at Indian Arrow Rapids, a most delightful experience. The river was shallow enough there for them to sit and let the current beat against their backs. The summer heat forgotten, they had splashed and frolicked like children in their square-necked, scalloped-skirted bathing suits with bloomers.

The Fourth had entailed a parade. Grace had watched the procession from the front porch with her aunt, both of them enjoying creamy homemade ice cream the Mosses had churned for their guests. There had been brass bands, clowns and jugglers, children in small wagons with dogs yipping after them, the local fireman's association, and buggies bedecked with red, white and blue bunting.

Grace heard that the local women always went to decorate the graves of their Confederate dead, and picnicked after the ceremony. But as an outsider she would never have thought of attending.

Now, dressed in a short-sleeved, bottle-green gown that bared her neck to the balmy evening, she stepped onto the upper porch outside Martha's room. So far she had avoided the dances in the hotel ballrooms. But tonight Martha insisted her niece join the festivities. Grace knew she would enjoy no peace until she did.

"There she is! What luck!" called a familiar and welcome voice. Below, Amelia stood on the side of the busy street, looking up at Grace. With her were two young men and another young woman. Grace waved to acknowledge them.

"Look what we have—fireworks!" She gestured to the bulging bag clasped by the dark-haired man at her side. Much more interesting to Grace, however, was the broadly smiling face above. It was easily one of the most handsome she had ever seen! "Come down, Grace! I promised to introduce you to some friends. Here they are!"

Grace leaned over the rail. "All right, I'll be right down."

Not even pausing in Martha's bedroom, she offered a hasty explanation and good night. She might not be going to the dance, but she *was* going out. Music blared on the ground floor. Suddenly Grace felt carefree and nervously excited.

The foursome was waiting for her next to the main door. Amelia was dancing from foot to foot like a ten-year-old. She introduced Grace to her companions. The handsome one was Daniel Monroe. Amelia mentioned his parents lived in Clarkesville; his father had ties to the local railroad and owned a woolen mill. The other gentleman, hardly shabby himself with his high cheekbones and blonde hair, was Trent Hargrove, brother of Alice Hargrove. The aforementioned Alice pressed near to Daniel as Grace was introduced, turning her sweet face with rosebud lips up to him.

"Now let's find a place to set those off. I've been waiting *all day*."

Daniel Monroe glanced apologetically at Grace, clearly aware they'd hardly had a chance to speak first. She encouraged him by saying, "Yes, let's."

"Well, I guess the street's the best place. Let's go down a bit from the hotel, though."

They found a relatively quiet side street. Trent set down his lantern, which coupled with the moon light gave Daniel enough illumination to unload his bag of goodies.

"Matches," he said, holding out a hand. Amelia complied. Before Grace could prepare herself, something whined and exploded near the feet of the ladies, shooting off light. They all jumped and squealed with the required amount of surprise.

"Oh, you just *had* to scare us!" exclaimed Alice. "Let's light the Chinese firecrackers."

Those created a great deal of noise, drawing a disgruntled old man to the porch of his nearby house.

Trent shrugged lamely. "What is The Fourth of July without a few fireworks?" he called.

Rather than confront them, the man went back inside. Daniel brought out some wand-like shapes and gave one to Amelia, saying they would make less noise. He explained that when he lit it, the wand would sparkle as Amelia held it at arm's length. She giggled as golden light spewed from the end. But Grace had to admit the sparks so near the women's voluminous skirts made her a bit nervous. When Daniel extended one to her, she hesitated.

"It will be all right," he encouraged her. "Dangerous as they appear, I've never known these to set anything afire."

He must have read her mind. She took the wand, and he lit it. Vibrant green fizzled from the end. She laughed, turning in slow circles like the other girls. The colors dazzled her eyes. When her dizzy gaze settled on Daniel Monroe, she saw that he was staring at her. A strand of his dark hair, which was parted on the side, fell softly over his forehead. She smiled. He smiled back. *Instant connection*, she thought. She stopped short of analyzing that.

After they set off a couple of Roman candles, the balls of fire shooting high up into the air and drawing passers-by, Daniel suggested they take a buggy ride. "That will give us a chance to get to know Miss Galveston," he said.

River Street was busy with traffic. People were going from one end of town to the other, partaking of the many celebrations occurring simultaneously. It was not difficult to wave down one of the many pleasure vehicles. As they climbed into the open carriage with seats facing seats, the driver asked, "Where to?"

"Just drive about, if you please."

The men sat on one side, the women on the other. Their skirts made it crowded, but Grace decided that was all right. She would have been much too nervous had she been crammed in beside the dark-haired young man who now faced her. As it was, she was having a hard time keeping her eyes off of him. It was hard to remember that there were other people in the carriage.

Daniel seemed eager to engage her in conversation. "So how are you enjoying your stay in Tallulah?" he asked.

"Very much, especially now that Miss Wylie has taken me under her wing." Grace smiled at her new friend. "We've been having lots of fun. I broke her in the first day with the hike to Hurricane Falls."

"You didn't," said Trent.

"I did! She complained less than you do. Oh, look, Grace, there's the bank. I think I told you Alice's and Trent's father manages it."

"No, you hadn't said."

"But she told us that you were an opera singer," Alice chimed in, leaning her golden head forward and fixing her slanted green eyes on Grace. "You must have a fine life. Do you live in one of those huge mansions on Fifth Avenue?"

"Alice," her brother said, protesting her presumption.

But Grace decided to answer her. "No, not hardly. Well, I have to admit my father does make his home in that area, but my aunt and I live independently in a modest brownstone fronting Gramercy Park. I have always lived there, since I was born. You see, my father remarried just after my mother passed away."

"Oh," said Alice thoughtfully, and a bit distastefully. "But...I thought Amelia said your family was of Southern stock?"

"I'm afraid there is not much left of my mother's side of the family."

Daniel cleared his throat when he saw Grace bite her lip. He said brightly, "I've been to New York once, as part of my graduation trip. We even went to the opera. My mother is a huge fan. She made us wait to go until Christmas so she could see a performance. Of course that was some years ago, when the opera was still housed in The Academy of Music."

"Ah, yes, I didn't really begin until the new building was up. I remember being in awe of Christine Nilsson as Marguerite in *Faust*. After that it's been nothing but Lilli Lehmann in German roles. But what else did you see while in New York?"

"The Metropolitan Museum of Art, of course." Daniel's eyes glowed with enthusiasm. "It was amazing."

"I agree, I don't care what all the people say who are mad that it keeps on expanding and crowding out Central Park. Of course the park is one of my favorite places, too, but to me it seems not a detraction, but—"

"A compliment!" Daniel finished her sentence.

"Yes, exactly."

He smiled in satisfaction. "There was an early freeze while we were there, and people were skating on the pond and sleighing through the park."

"Oh, it sounds like so much fun," cried Amelia, breaking into the exchange.

Remembering their companions, Daniel and Grace sat back a bit. Grace glanced at Amelia. "I wouldn't know. Monsieur LeMonte will hardly let me outside in the winter. I guess he's afraid my vocal chords will freeze." She laughed a bit tightly. "I have to be resigned to hearing the sleigh bells as they speed past."

"How sad!"

"Tallulah is quite beautiful even in winter," Daniel told her. "There's nothing like the ice and snow on the mountains. If I've seen New York in the snow, maybe one day you'll get to see Tallulah Falls all covered in white." He smiled in a way that made Grace's heart flip.

"I'd like that."

"And we'd all like it if you'd come to our church on

Sunday…Trinity Episcopal, up on the hill. Lots of the tourists go there."

"I don't see why not."

Alice, who was starting to look petulant over her exclusion, took the opportunity to claim Daniel's attention. She started discussing the grave decorating that had occurred earlier that day. She had taken roses and a flag to the grave of Major-Somebody, probably her distinguished grandfather, Grace thought. They were passing The Robinson House, but Grace wasn't interested in the throngs of people surrounding the brightly-lit inn. Nor would she let Alice's comments about how moving it had been to honor their Southern defenders, and how *that* was what meant something to her about the holiday, bother her. Instead she subtly turned her attention to the man across from her.

Daniel Monroe intrigued her. His clothes were not new, but were of good quality. His features were aristocratic, but he was so unaffected. His jaw was strong and his brows straight, but there was a gentleness and keen perception she sensed and was drawn by. He was so very different from the dandies to whom she was accustomed, with their British-styled mannerisms—even different from Blake. She realized he had spoken very little of himself. Grace determined that she would be the one to ask questions next time they met.

* * *

They were going to be late. And it was all due to her aunt's malingering over tea. Grace tapped her foot impatiently.

"Aunt, we must go now!" she exclaimed. She flung a hand toward the open window. "See, there's the church bell!"

With a sigh Martha patted her lips with her linen napkin. Grace knew the reason for her indifference. Back in New York, Martha was plenty sharp about morals and church attendance, but that was due in greater part to her desire to see and be seen than to any real religious devotion. While she was on vacation, she clearly felt there was no such need for posturing.

35

Grace was ready to throw all respect to the wind and head out the door without her when Martha finally rose and reached for her parasol. Outside Grace set as brisk a pace as her skirts would allow, aiming for the small white church on the hill above. She could see people filing in. By the time they arrived everyone was seated.

"Hmm," said Martha in approval of the surprisingly gracious interior.

Looking around, Grace spotted Amelia with her family several rows up, but no Daniel. Amelia turned and waved. But all the seats were taken save a few spots in the back. Grace and Martha slid into a pew.

"So," Martha whispered, "where is this young man you nearly broke my neck with haste getting here to see?"

Unable to answer, Grace studied the crowd again. No, he definitely wasn't present. And he had seemed so eager to meet her again! The pianist had begun to play. Her heart sank with disappointment.

Then a side door near the front of the sanctuary opened. Daniel! Prepared to overlook his tardy and unconventional entrance in her pleasure to see him, she curved her lips into a smile of welcome. But he wasn't looking for her. Then she noticed he wore a white robe over his dark suit and carried a large Bible. Grace's mouth fell open in a most unladylike gesture as Daniel Monroe walked right up to the platform in front of the congregation and sat down in the big, carved oak chair!

Chapter Four

Daniel did try not to focus overmuch on the presence of Grace Galveston in the church service. He was always aware of the need, during the prayers and singing, to worship and prepare his heart to deliver the morning's message. His routine was to pray for his own decrease so the presence of the Lord might increase. Doing so was always necessary in light of the half dozen dewy-eyed teenage girls who never failed to line the front pew, and doubly—no, exponentially—so with the glorious red-haired angel present. This time, because of Grace, he was asking for the proper focus for *himself*. The one direct glance at her he did allow himself met with her raised eyebrow. Uh-oh.

He did also notice that during the hymn "This Is My Father's World," she was not singing, but writing something in a tiny notebook. Hmm.

Daniel concentrated on the message God had given to him for that week. Some of those present would not warm to it, he knew. When he had been appointed to the newly built church here in Tallulah Falls, it had been with the understanding that it would draw not only the residents of the town, but wealthy vacationers as well. His own background had made him the ideal candidate to fill Trinity's pulpit. And in the last few years, he had found that in the relaxed atmosphere of a summer retreat many tourists were indeed more open to spiritual truths.

Standing at the pulpit, he directed the congregation's attention to Matthew 19:16-30, the story of the rich young ruler. The text which he read aloud detailed how that man had come to Jesus asking what he should do to receive eternal life. The fact that he had called Jesus "Good Teacher" had given the Lord the perfect opportunity to point out: "There is none good but one, that is, God." Then he had encouraged the young ruler to obey the commandments—avoiding adultery, lying, stealing, murder, and also honoring one's parents and loving one's neighbor. These things the ruler had done.

"But he *knew* something was missing," Daniel told his listeners. "He knew the truth of what God had said, the lack of goodness within himself. For he asked, 'What lack I yet?'"

Some fashionably attired individuals, including Grace's aunt, shifted in their seats. But the eyes of most were fastened on Daniel's face.

"Have you ever looked inside and known there was an emptiness—and something holding you back from God? Jesus knew this young man's dilemma. For He replied, 'If thou wilt be perfect, go and sell that thou hast, and give to the poor, and thou shalt have treasure in heaven: and come and follow Me.' The Lord knew this was the one thing the man was unwilling to do, for he had allowed his money to tie him to earth and its pleasures. Thus, the young man went away sorrowful."

Daniel went on to share from the Scriptures how Jesus had explained to His disciples that it was hard for the rich to enter heaven, because one must be willing to leave homes, lands and families, to take up one's cross and follow Him. He told the congregation that it was not wrong to have money—that he knew many who did, and who loved the Lord wholeheartedly, and were a great blessing to the less fortunate.

"Financial abundance can be a gift," he said, "rather like a Christian heritage—or the ability to lead—or a beautiful voice."

He smiled slightly, catching sight of Miss Galveston's brown eyes.

"And like all gifts, it is at its greatest when used to the glory of God, and as He intends. The point the Lord was making was that the issue lies with the attitude of our hearts. No possessions, no experiences, no talents, can fill the void created by the Lord. Nothing can but Himself. We must hold all other things in life lightly, placing them in subjection to His sovereignty, *willing* to let them go if need be. Realizing that fulfillment comes only through a personal relationship with Jesus."

Daniel flipped the pages of his well-worn Bible. "In closing, I'd like to share a verse from Proverbs 13—number seven." Slowly he read, "'There is that maketh himself rich, yet hath nothing: there is that maketh himself poor, yet hath great riches.'"

After the service, Daniel stood at the front door. He had removed his robe to appear less formal as he spoke to each departing parishioner. Grace Galveston and her aunt, having lingered in conversation with the Wylies, were among the last to exit. Even before he saw Grace's very intentional expression, Daniel knew exactly what she would say. He decided to let manners fly to the four winds and head it right off.

Taking Grace's proffered hand, he said, "I don't blame you one bit for what you are surely thinking of me, but before you write me off forever as deceptive and unfeeling, *please* allow me an opportunity to explain. Say, a stroll this afternoon?"

She chewed her full lower lip and contemplated him. He put all the little boy pleading into his face that he could muster. But before she could answer, her aunt surprised him by questioning, "Daniel *Monroe*? Not related to the Monroes of Darien, Georgia?"

He turned astonished eyes on the stately woman. "Why, yes, ma'am. And once again I am sadly lacking in manners, for I should have—"

"Given me an opportunity to introduce my aunt, Martha Hampton," Grace finished for him.

"Yes."

He reached for Miss Hampton's gloved hand, intending to bow over it, but Martha gave a sniff and impatiently waved off his

39

attempt. Then, unexpectedly, she tapped him with her parasol. "You'll join us for luncheon at The Cliff House and explain all." Up snapped the parasol, cloaking her in regal shade.

Her tone would brook no argument. Besides, it was just the opportunity Daniel had wanted. He jumped into motion. "Please give me just a minute to close up the church, and I will escort you ladies to the inn."

"You were only an infant when the war began, and you had an older brother named James. Your parents were fine Christian people. Having come from money, you at least have some entitlement to speak about the subject," said Martha over a fine congealed salad, as if having come to these conclusions as they walked to The Cliff House and were seated in its dining room.

Both of the young people stared at her.

"Well, don't look at me like I'm a soothsayer." She laughed. "All that is if my memory serves me correctly and your parents were indeed owners of a plantation outside Darien."

Daniel recovered himself. "It's true. In fact, my brother still lives there. The land is sharecropped now, but he stays busy overseeing things, including our own portion, and our small shipping business. But, forgive me…I'm at a loss…"

"My father was acquainted very informally with yours. He was the owner of Hampton Hall outside Savannah. All the planter families knew the other planters and the cotton factors up and down the coast." Martha leaned to her right to allow a waiter to deliver the main course.

"Naturally my memories of the war years are very few, really up until the time my father decided to cut most of his losses and move us to our summer home in Clarkesville. I was about six or seven then. But, yes…I do think Hampton Hall sounds vaguely familiar." Daniel paused, cocking his head to one side. "I believe my father once said it was a terrible shame that it was among those burned, for it was one of the finest on the coast."

"It was," Martha agreed readily, eyes on the meat she was cutting.

"And the land, is it still in your family?"

"Sold for back taxes." Martha's knife slipped out of her fingers and fell to her plate. With a rigid jaw she said, "This beef is far too tough. The roast at Del Monicoe's always melts in one's mouth."

"Cantankerous old cow," Daniel quipped.

Martha gave a quick, unplanned bark of laughter that caused Grace to look at her in amazement. He decided it was a good idea to keep the conversation moving along.

"Well, now I am more sure than ever about the invitation I had already planned to extend today! I had already mentioned to you, Miss Galveston, what an avid opera fan my mother is—and herself an accomplished musician. If she learned that I had made the acquaintance of a Metropolitan Opera singer and failed to bring her for a visit, I would never hear the end of it. And now, also knowing that our families have this connection...well, what do you ladies say? I had planned a visit home this week. Will you accompany me?"

A tiny frown of uncertainty flitted over Martha's face. Grace's reaction was quite different. She had been both patient and attentive during the exchange of the last few minutes, but now she directed the conversation back to what was clearly to her the most pressing matter at hand. "I could hardly say at this point. I am still waiting to hear why you invited me to church but failed to tell me you were the minister."

"Uh...yes." How to share the truth without sounding immodest...? Daniel tapped a finger on his unused dessert fork. "I'm very sorry about that. Well, sort of. You see, I was so enjoying the evening we met, and how naturally everything was flowing. You know how when people find out you're an opera singer, things sometimes change? Well, in a strange way, being a minister is rather similar. You let it out of the bag, and the next thing you know people stop acting like themselves. Only, around me they get all stiff and careful."

Grace's laughter pealed forth, a lovely musical sound that seemed to race down his spine like...like a finger over piano keys. He sat up straight in response and smiled. "I can imagine it might be like that," she said, nodding. "I can imagine all too well."

He grinned, relieved. "Also...I didn't want you to come to the service because you felt obligated, invited by the minister and all."

She said nothing, just met his eyes with the smile still lingering about her lips. But the implication was clear. He had wanted her to come just because she had liked him and wanted to see him again.

The moment was broken as Martha asked, "So, if your parents live in Clarkesville and your church is here, where do you live?"

"I was a permanent boarder of Mr. Young's before his hotel burned. Oh, not The Grand View," he inserted quickly, seeing their startled expressions, "the Young's Hotel, or The Tallulah. It was on the upper gorge overlooking Indian Arrow Rapids. If you drive by the site now you'll see it's being rebuilt. But I decided I needed something more—stable. I was able to find a small house in town for a good deal."

Thick slices of shortcake topped with cream and fresh strawberries arrived.

"Mmm," said Grace.

But Martha sighed. "Really, I don't think I can. That beef quite wore me out." She didn't laugh along with the others and appeared suddenly drained. "I'd like a nap now. I think I'll retire to my room."

Daniel stood with her. "About that invitation . . ?"

The ladies glanced at one another. Grace nodded. "Very well," said Martha. "We would be pleased to accept. I'll let you arrange all the details with my niece."

"Thank you, ma'am. My family will be delighted." He held out her chair and caught her eye as she moved back from the table. "With your permission, I was hoping to take Miss Galveston to see the view from Lover's Leap this afternoon. That is, if she is so inclined."

"Oh, wonderful," said Grace. "You can tell me the legend about the spot."

"That is fine. I'll send down our maid to accompany you. Good afternoon, Mr. Monroe...I mean, Rev. Monroe." Martha smiled stiffly. "My, that will take some getting used to—you don't look old enough to be out of college yet."

After the older woman had gone, Daniel sat back down. He enjoyed the sensation of being alone with Grace, and watching her savor her dessert. Their solitude was short-lived, though, for when he sallied proudly into the lobby with Grace on his arm, he saw a young maid waiting to follow them on their walk. At least she kept a discreet distance behind them so that, while they were properly chaperoned, she could not hear everything they said.

"Of course you know all these lands once belonged to the Cherokee," Daniel told Grace as they strolled south on the hotel grounds. She nodded. "Many stories have grown up from that time. It's said that the Cherokee rarely ventured into the gorge."

"Why not?" she asked.

"They held it in awe. Some of them believed it was inhabited by a race of little people known as Yunwi Tsundi. They were supposed to live in caves and under the falls and kidnap women and children...who never returned."

"How strange. I love to hear Indian lore."

"Well, since you're encouraging me, there's another tale of a mysterious Indian maiden who led an infatuated warrior to a high cave. Strange supernatural things befell him. When he awoke, he was in the forest and could find no trace of the cave or the girl. When he returned to his people, he found he had been missing for many years. He didn't listen to the girl's warning to not talk about his experience. When he was questioned he revealed it all. Right away he fell ill and died within a week."

"My, you know a lot about these things, for a minister," Grace teased.

Daniel set a slow pace as they descended the trail towards Lover's Leap, aware his companion still wore her Sunday finery. He grinned and helped her over a fallen log...a wonderful excuse to briefly hold her hand. "You can't live in these parts and *not* know. Now Amelia, she's home grown. I don't have her bragging rights."

At Grace's questioning look, he explained. "Her folks have been in these parts forever. She's Scotch-Irish, English, and a drop Cherokee."

"*Really?*" Grace was fascinated. She visualized Amelia's glossy dark hair and, remembering cheekbones that could definitely be considered high, nodded with recognition. That explained Amelia's bond to the land. It must be wonderful to have such a sense of belonging, she thought. She stopped walking as her eye fell on a grouping of large boulders in the forest ahead.

"That's Council Rocks," Daniel offered, following her gaze. "Ties in to the legend of Lover's Leap. They say many years ago a young white hunter was captured and was held prisoner there, where the Indians liked to meet. A beautiful Indian girl named—you guessed it—Tallulah—fell in love with him. But her father sentenced him to be thrown into the gorge from what's now called Lover's Leap."

"Let me guess again…she jumped after him?"

"Your romantic heart has discerned the truth, or should I say, the legend."

Grace laughed. She saw that up ahead there was a slight thinning of the trees. A young man about Daniel's age was bending over a large black box secured on stilts, a tripod. Daniel smiled at the wonderful timing and called out, "Hello, Walter!"

The man swung around to look at them. "Oh, hello, Daniel."

Daniel introduced Walter Hunicutt to Grace and watched him take her in with surprise. He knew Daniel did not often go about with young women. "Walter can often be seen with this camera of his, capturing images of our town and the gorge…that is, when he's not making his twig furniture or painting," Daniel explained.

"My, how talented you must be."

Walter shrugged depreciatingly. "Been thinking about doing a series of postcards."

"A wonderful idea," Daniel agreed. "Bet you'd sell a million. You just setting up here?"

"I'm ready to shoot the view from the leap."

"I take it you want it without people?"

Walter looked thoughtful. "I had thought so, but not necessarily. People do make it seem real. I've already taken one from down the cliffs, showing the precipice itself. So, I suppose the two of you would make good subjects."

Grace was inching up on the overlook as he spoke. When she took in the sheer drop below, she shivered and hurried back a few steps, her hand at her heart. The men laughed.

Feeling a bit bad for manipulating Walter's good manners and turning what probably would have been a view of the gorge into a view of himself and Grace, he whispered in Walter's ear, "Pay ya later."

Under his moustache, Walter grinned lopsidedly and waved aside his words. It was not hard to see why Daniel would want to make the most of the opportunity. He backed up his large format, wooden dry-plate camera and directed the couple to stand with their backs to the gorge, Grace on Daniel's arm. Within moments, their images were captured for eternity, together.

"Come by later this week and pick up the picture," Walter said.

Daniel thanked him. While Walter inconspicuously packed up his equipment, Daniel found a large rock for himself and Grace to sit upon. The maid found another rock within view. Quietly he said, "I hope your aunt was not too upset."

"Why should she be?" Grace turned to him, her earrings dancing.

"Well, me bringing up the past and all. Clearly it was a very painful time for her. I am curious about one thing, though, if you'll permit me…" He waited for Grace to nod. "How did she end up in New York City?"

Grace sighed. "I've heard the tale so many times, but it still wrings my heart. My grandfather was already very ill at the end of the war. Most of the slaves had left, and he had taken on too much physical labor for his age. Even after a fever had left him weakened, he continued at the pace of a much younger man. When the Yankees came, it caused his demise. They burned the house. Days later, Grandfather died in one of the cabins. My mother and aunt were forced to flee into Savannah. They had to stay with a cold-hearted great uncle who was none too pleased to have more mouths to feed."

She told him how Hampton Galveston had arrived in Savannah in January of 1865, a young physician under the red and blue silk banners of the 131st New York Volunteer Infantry. While on duty in the beleaguered, captured city, he one day encountered a beautiful red-haired girl weeping on the steps of the military hospital, unable to find any work. Something about her had stirred his pity and his passion. When his regiment was mustered out of service in July, he had taken Louisa, along with her older spinster sister Martha and her maid Sally, home to New York.

"But that was a mistake," Grace almost whispered, even though the maid had opened a small book and begun to read, paying them little heed. Daniel leaned forward, attuned to her emotions. "His wealthy parents raised such a commotion at the arrival of his penniless Rebel bride that he was forced to set up housekeeping in a modest brownstone. He supported them by his own earnings."

She swallowed, looking at the tips of her boots. "Then, my mother died in childbirth, my father unable to save her. He was demoralized. His parents saw that there was still the opportunity for him to make a brilliant society match, if he would but separate himself from the past and keep things quiet—"

"—Miss Galveston," Daniel interrupted. "You don't have to—"

"No, it's all right," she said hastily. "There's no sense in being mysterious." She turned her moist caramel eyes upon him and laughed shakily. "But you might as well call me Grace if I'm telling you all this."

He made bold to take her hand. "I'm honored." Her hand trembled ever-so-slightly, which did strange things inside his chest.

She continued, "So he moved back home. Soon after, he married and began another family. Ever since he has financially supported my aunt and me, but we rarely saw him until—until recently. His parents passed away some time ago, and that along with his wise investments in newspaper and railroads has meant that money is no issue for him."

Daniel sensed the hurt about which she was not ready to speak. How could a man virtually abandon such a lovely, innocent child? Had he no idea what kind of scars he could leave? He wanted to take her in his arms but contented himself with merely patting her hand. He cleared his throat. "I—uh—do feel I understand much more now. Thank you."

She looked into his eyes. The moment was made all the more powerful by her silence. It was as if she were searching for something. He found himself wanting to give it, whatever it was. Finally she said, "I liked your sermon this morning."

He waited for further comment or question. When none came, he chuckled lightly and asked, "Does that mean I'm truly forgiven?"

"If you promise to be utterly honest from this moment forward."

He could have made a joke about her binding a preacher to truthfulness. Instead, he said, "I do."

"I also liked the song." Unexpectedly she jumped up. She started walking toward the overlook. "I've heard it once before. I wrote down the words so I wouldn't forget them. They are so appropriate for this place. I just have to laugh at the Darwinists. How could anyone ever believe that all this just evolved?"

She gazed over the gorge, the breeze lifting her skirts and her amazing hair. How could anyone believe *she* had just evolved? Suddenly she began to sing, and the sound—so clear, so pure— transfixed him.

This is my Father's world, and to my listening ears
All nature sings, and round me rings the music of the spheres.
This is my Father's world: I rest me in the thought
Of rocks and trees, of skies and seas—His hand the wonders wrought.

This is my Father's world, oh, let me ne'er forget
That though the wrong seems oft so strong, God is the ruler yet.
This is my Father's world: why should my heart be sad?
The Lord is King: let the heavens ring! God reigns: let the earth be glad!

When she finished, silence fell. Daniel noticed even the birds were quiet. As her voice had spiraled into the words "This is my Father's world: why should my heart be sad?" there had been such hope, and such wistfulness in her tone, that his own heart had squeezed tight. Too, there had been such visions in his head of the sparkling world of the opera and the city from which she had come, and for which she was surely destined, that now he had to remind himself of his own words from earlier that day. He had seen the person she was before being awestruck by her voice, and he must keep that in mind.

She turned around, her hands clasped before her chest, her cheeks flushed. "There, I did it," she exclaimed with pleasure.

"Uh—was there ever any doubt that you could?" he questioned.

"Why, yes." Grace walked toward him in a fashion that illustrated her name. "You know I'm here to rest my voice, and that's no joke. There was a role last season that—well, changed things. There has been a lot of pressure, lots of rehearsals, preparations for the fall. It started to tell on me. I lost my breathing. My nerves were getting the better of me. There was one particularly awful moment and well...here I am."

"I can't wait for my mother to meet you," he blurted, and then colored like a boy when he realized how it sounded. But he was rewarded by another of those beautiful peals of laughter.

She was amazing, fascinating, one moment vulnerable and open, the next, seemingly untouchable. Daniel realized he could not remember ever being this intrigued by a woman. His mother *would* have questions. And he knew he had much yet to learn about where Grace Galveston stood with God. *Lord,* he prayed silently, *I really like this woman. I mean, I really,* really *like her. Help me to be wise.*

As if the seriousness of his thoughts were betrayed by his face, Grace, too, sobered. "About that," she said. "What would you think of Amelia Wylie coming along?"

"Miss Wylie?"

"Yes, don't you think she would really enjoy an outing?"

"I—I guess so..." Had he scared her off? He knew Grace and Amelia were fast becoming friends, but he was surprised and—he must admit—a bit disappointed that Grace wanted to invite her. Oh, well. Best to put a good face on it. He straightened and forced cheer into his tone. "We'll have a wonderful time."

Chapter Five

The morning of their overnight trip to Clarkesville, Grace spent more time than usual in front of the mirror. With Maureen's help she created an elaborate coiffure. Clad in a traveling gown with a stand-up collar and dropped waist, hues of peach, tan and chocolate contrasting smartly in plaid and solids, she made her way to the depot. The light in Daniel's eyes when he saw her was well worth all the effort. Amelia, who was waiting beside him, gave Grace an excited hug.

Something about the Rev. Daniel Monroe had caused Grace to open up and talk about herself at their previous meetings. It was not something she easily did. That very vulnerability she felt had been the catalyst for her suggestion that Amelia's stabilizing presence be included on their little trip. And now, she was determined to learn more about Daniel—before they arrived at his parents' home!

The train had scarcely left the station when she said, "I'd love to hear what prompted you to become a minister."

"Prompted me? Why, I guess that would be—God." He grinned as the others laughed. "But to answer you more fully, I had an uncle who was a minister. When I was a child he had a great deal of influence on me. Since I, like him, was a second son, my parents did not protest my decision when I told them I felt God's call on my life."

"You think they would have had you been the older son?"
Daniel thought a moment. "It might have made things more difficult if James had resisted working in the family business. But my parents love the Lord and I like to think they would have found a way for me to pursue my calling."

"Do you ever wish for a larger church, in a larger city?" That was Martha's question.

Daniel shook his head. "Tallulah is home. I can't see myself being anywhere else. Of course," he added with a smile, "God's plans and ours don't always match up. I hope I'll always be in step with Him, willing to go where He leads."

Aunt Martha's brow rose imperiously. "With that outlook you may end up in the Appalachian wilderness somewhere, or in Africa!"

But Daniel only chuckled. "You are right, ma'am."

Grace fell silent at this. She did not wish to reveal that her feelings on this particular subject ran more parallel to Martha's than Daniel's. She certainly did not live for New York City society like her aunt, but she did enjoy its conveniences.

She was also puzzled by Daniel's references to his relationship with God…as though God spoke to him openly and frequently. She couldn't imagine having a human father that involved in the details of one's life, much less a heavenly one. Somehow she knew Daniel wasn't being merely braggadocios, though. That just wasn't the way he was. And the way he was made her want to know more.

That brought Grace to her motives. Clearly she was attracted to Daniel, so to be honest with herself she must admit that she desired more than a summer friendship. At least she thought she did. But Daniel had just said he had no desire to leave Tallulah, and her life was in the process of unfolding in New York. Everyone had seemed to believe that life should include the cultured Blake Greene. But he seemed so far away right now, and Daniel was so near, his handsome face turning toward her with the most heart-stopping smile. Grace decided to put the "buts" and "ifs" far from her and merely enjoy this interlude.

She smiled in return. "Is James your only sibling?"

"Oh, goodness, no…you mean I've entirely failed to mention my sister?"

Grace nodded. Amelia giggled.

"I'm hoping you can meet her at dinner tonight, along with her husband and daughter."

"You have a niece?"

"I do." Daniel fairly glowed with pride, as if he had something to do with this amazing fact. "Her name is Melanie. She's two years old. My sister's name is Emily Anne."

"Her husband, Mark Taylor, is a judge," Amelia added.

The train began to slow.

"We're approaching Clarkesville. The depot is a bit of a ride from the town, and my parents' home, so they will have sent a carriage," Daniel told them.

Grace was glad. The July morning had rapidly begun to heat up, and the inside of the passenger car was growing stuffy. She was quite unaccustomed to the southern humidity, a foe to be reckoned with even near the mountains.

As they disembarked the train, Grace was surprised to see a grand open carriage drawn by two gleaming black horses and sporting a family crest on the side. Even Aunt Martha looked impressed. A somber Negro man stepped down from his perch to open the vehicle's door for them. "Mornin', Mist' Daniel," he said.

Daniel grinned at him warmly as he handed the ladies up. "Good to see you again, Abe."

Once their valises were loaded, they set off at a leisurely pace, parasols shading them from the sun. Daniel had their driver take a round-about route to allow them a brief tour of the town. Clarkesville had quite a different feeling from Tallulah. Tallulah's appeal came from its newer buildings and, of course, the mountain views and gorge. If Grace had not known better, she would have guessed that Clarkesville was nestled in the heartlands rather than perched on the edge of the Appalachians. Mature trees shaded grand ante-bellum homes set back among green lawns. Daniel pointed out several with comments like, "Minis Hall, 1848," and "Gloaming Cottage, built by

Jarvis Van Buren, a cousin of the past president…the second story was added about 1870." Daniel explained that Van Buren had been behind the building of both the Presbyterian Church and Grace Episcopal Church. As they passed this lovely white structure with its tall, green-shuttered, multi-paned windows, Daniel told them that his family had long rented a box pew inside. There were also a number of hotels in town. Clarkesville had been considered the "jumping off" point for visitors to Tallulah and also to Toccoa Falls before the railroad had been completed. Grace glimpsed a brick courthouse on the town square before they turned up another side street.

"And at last…Crown Pointe," Daniel said, gesturing ahead as they entered a narrow drive between brick pillars. "My father named the house thus, saying it was the jewel in the crown of all he owned, mainly because it was always the family's favorite retreat."

Grace leaned forward and gasped. "Why, it's beautiful!"

"It reminds me of Hampton Hall," said Martha in a strangled voice. Grace glanced at her. There were tears in her eyes, and her face twisted as she sought to contain sudden emotion. "Grace, this is much the sight that would have greeted you near Savannah, had our home been standing."

Imagining how Martha must feel, Grace ventured to place her hand over her aunt's. To her added amazement, Martha did not withdraw.

"How I wish…" she whispered.

Grace's attention was turned by the appearance of a couple on the front porch—Daniel's parents. They were waving to him, and he to them. The carriage drew up right in front of the house. As Grace alighted and mounted the steps between the two middle columns, she had a keen taste of what the life of the Southern aristocracy had been before the war…a life that had once been Martha's. She took her aunt's arm, understanding her a little more.

"Miss Hampton, Miss Galveston, may I present my parents, Mr. and Mrs. William Monroe. Father and mother, I'm pleased to introduce Miss Martha Hampton, her niece Miss Grace Galveston— and of course you know Miss Wylie."

Grace curtsied deeply. It was suddenly very important that these people think well of her. She glanced up to see a knowing smile on the lovely older woman's face. Reddish-brown hair was swept back into a simple, old-fashioned style. Tiny creases marked the corners of Mrs. Monroe's eyes as she smiled. Her bustled gown emphasized a still-trim figure.

It was apparent that Daniel's dark good looks came from his father, although Mr. Monroe's hair and moustache were now liberally sprinkled with gray. Of the two, the elder man was slightly the shorter. He bowed to the visitors.

Mrs. Monroe took Aunt Martha's hand, then Grace's. "We are so happy you've come to visit. I've been able to think of nothing else since Daniel told me of you. And of course, Miss Wylie, your company never fails to be a delight." She turned to the blushing young woman and gave her cheek a quick kiss.

"Thank you for having us," said Martha somewhat stiffly.

"Crown Pointe has reminded Miss Hampton of her girlhood home near Savannah," Daniel mentioned, smiling gently.

"Ah, yes! Of course Daniel told us about that. I can't wait to talk about it all. We'll show you to your rooms, then I thought we could have luncheon on the veranda. The breeze makes it cool there, even most afternoons."

Inside, a curving staircase rose from a spacious entrance hall and wrapped around a brass chandelier. As they ascended, Mrs. Monroe explained that they could offer two guest rooms, one with twin beds. She asked if this would be comfortable. They assured her it would. Grace and Amelia decided to share the one room. This actually made things more interesting for Grace, who had never had the experience of giggling and whispering secrets at bedtime with a sister or friend. She was just girlish enough still to sometimes wish for such exchanges.

* * *

Lunch had been an enjoyable affair consisting of delicious, cool foods and light conversation. They had spoken of the generalities of their lives, common acquaintances and events they shared from the past, and the pleasures of Martha's and Grace's visit in Tallulah. The congenial atmosphere continued after they had all rested and gathered again for dinner. Judge Taylor had arrived with his family around five. Daniel's sister had proven gracious and was as fashionably dressed as Grace, who wore an ice blue taffeta moiré dinner dress. Two-year-old Melanie Taylor had hurtled herself into Daniel's arms and squealed as he tossed her into the air. Grace watched the exchange, smiling.

"I'm afraid she's a little wound up," Emily Anne apologized. "She was so excited about seeing 'Uncle Danny' today that she wouldn't take her nap."

"We're hoping the excitement continues to overpower crankiness," Judge Taylor added wryly, dropping his walking stick into a brass container near the door. He cut a fine figure in his black frock coat, Grace noticed.

"Oh, dear," Daniel exclaimed, ignoring everybody else and holding the child out like a rag doll. "No nap? You won't get cranky, will you?" The little girl shook her head and pursed her cherubic lips for a kiss. Daniel smacked them loudly and said, "Never!"

Grace found herself laughing.

The adorable child was trundled off to have her meal in the kitchen, protesting tearfully, as the adults filed into the dining room. There, candles gleamed enchantingly on a Chippendale table set with white roses and silver. Servants quickly brought the first course and served it on Mrs. Monroe's blue and white floral china.

"These plates are lovely," commented Martha. "1820s Spode Filigree. I've been wondering, how did you come to save so many of your holdings, your possessions, despite the war? I remember hearing Darien was burned to the ground by black troops in June of 1863, well before Savannah's demise."

"It was indeed," agreed Mr. Monroe. "And not an event my family will ever forget."

Mrs. Monroe picked up his thread of conversation. "Mr. Monroe was not at home, of course. He had always been a member of The

McIntosh Light Dragoons, which eventually became The First Battalion and then part of the 5th Regiment, Georgia Cavalry." There was a trace of pride in her voice.

"I served on the coast for quite some time before we were shipped to Mississippi under Wheeler. Wounded in the Atlanta campaign," he added, flexing his arm, "and can still feel the effects of that. I was mad as fire to be laid up in the hospital there while Sherman razed our state and turned back to take Savannah."

"Anyway, dear, the burning of Darien..." Mrs. Monroe redirected.

"Yes, of course, go ahead."

Evelyn Monroe looked at Martha. "Our home was spared because it was occupied by Yankee officers."

"Oh!"

"Do you remember, Daniel? Emily Anne?"

"I hid him in the coal hole when they first rode up," Daniel's sister said.

"Thank you so much. I nearly choked to death—much less a glorious way to perish than at the hand of the Yankees," Daniel replied with mock indignation.

"I was trying to be helpful."

"So you do remember?" his mother asked.

He nodded. "Only vaguely, though. After being rescued from the coal hole, I remember having to stay in one of the tabby houses while the Yankees were there, and everybody acting calm and saying we must be very polite. But I could tell y'all were scared to death."

Evelyn sighed. "That we were."

"They could see the smoke of Darien 15 miles away on St. Simons," Mr. Monroe told them. "The amazing thing is, like Atlanta, she's recovered. Goes to show our resilience as a people. Where once we shipped out cotton, now we're one of the largest lumber shipping ports on the southern coast."

"And thus, your shipping business, directed by your son James, still flourishes," Grace concluded with a smile.

"That, along with Mr. Monroe's business investments locally, have kept us from the genteel poverty to which so many of our friends were reduced," Evelyn admitted. She smiled at her son. "During the off-season Daniel helps his father oversee the mill."

William added, "Many of the people who built summer homes in this area had to sell them. Things have not been the same since."

"Fortune has truly been with you," Grace said.

"Not merely fortune, Miss Galveston, but as we see it, the Lord's blessing," Mr. Monroe replied. He bowed his head slightly. "If you'll forgive the contradiction."

Grace did feel somewhat belittled, as if he were pointing out her lack of spiritual insight. Something rose within her. "Was it also the Lord's blessing that caused your prosperity before the war...or was it the labor of your slaves?"

Martha turned bright red. She hastened to say, "Please forgive her. She's spent her whole life in a Northern city, and has no idea how things were in the South."

Grace looked down at her plate, angry inside yet realizing that even if she were right, she had spoken rudely to Daniel's father, her host. She could not bear to look at Daniel.

William Monroe held up a hand. "No, indeed. I'm sure I sounded more pompous than I meant to. And what Miss Galveston asks now centers on the best question of this century. As I'm sure you know from our son—" he glanced at Daniel—"we are a Christian family. I did inherit my father's slaves. I always believed in gradual emancipation, that a slow process could best equip the black race with the skills necessary to live as free people in society. But while I owned them, no matter how good a relationship we had, or how benevolent a master I was, even teaching them Christianity, my conscience could not rest. In my heart I knew I was permitting an inexcusable wrong. I only knew peace after the war, which it seems God used to bring about His own will."

"His own will?" Martha asked in a choked voice. "For so many innocent people to suffer and die, to be dispossessed?"

"Oh, dear. Now we've caused both of you upset. We must seem heartless to go on so, in light of your experiences, Miss Hampton,"

Evelyn said, her own eyes suddenly filling with tears of compassion. "God can use even the most disastrous of events. I think that is what my father meant," Daniel said. "And *that* touches on perhaps the greatest question of all time—why God allows suffering. Of course, as I'm sure we all know—but still at times forget—it's that He allows humans a choice. Because of that, there is evil in the world. But difficulties can produce character, if we allow."

"Now we've done it," groaned Emily Anne, rolling her eyes as she raised her napkin to her lips. "We've gone and got him preaching. Mother's lemon layer cake will go completely unappreciated."

"It's my fault," said Grace.

"Nonsense." Daniel smiled at her.

Judge Taylor announced, "I for one stand ready to appreciate cake."

Everyone broke into laughter, the tension dispelled.

After they finished the meal, Evelyn clearly aimed to extend the renewed good cheer by shooing them into the parlor. She asked if Grace might now sing something for them. Feeling penitent for the dinner discussion and touched by William Monroe's humble words, she agreed before Aunt Martha could speak. To her surprise, Daniel slid onto the bench with a flourish and started thumbing through a music book.

"You play?" Grace asked.

"A bit. Not like my mother, but good enough for…oh, 'Rose of Killarney,' if that suits you."

Grace nodded.

Emily Anne clapped her hands with glee. "Oh, this is so exciting. I've never heard a real opera star before!"

"Not a star—" began Grace.

But Daniel cut her off. Firmly he contradicted, "A *star*." His eyes met hers and she blushed.

"You've sung for Daniel?" Amelia questioned. "When? I missed it?"

Daniel tried to downplay the event. "We took a walk after church, and she was so inspired by my preaching that she burst into song!"

Grace hit his shoulder playfully. "And what a song it was!" He pretended to reel drunkenly.

"Just a hymn from the service." Grace glanced back over her shoulder, embarrassed. Daniel's mother was watching carefully. Daniel's fingers rippled over the keys. She sang the first verse by herself, easily capturing every note, then she was surprised again. Daniel started to sing with her on the second. He had a fine baritone.

My heart is a nest that is robbed and forsaken
When gone from my sight is the girl that I love!
One word from your lips can my gladness awaken,
Your smile is the smile of the angels above!
Then meet me at twilight beside the bright waters,
The love that I've told you, I'd whisper once more;
Oh, sweetest and fairest of Erin's fair daughters,
Dear rose of Kilarney, Ma-rour-neen Astore!

The room burst into applause. Grace was so distracted by Daniel's gaze that she hardly noticed. Her attention was reclaimed as Evelyn said, "At lunch you were telling us how you were trained in the *bel canto* technique, Miss Galveston."

"Yes." Grace smiled at her.

"Would you feel up to something a bit more challenging?"

"What did you have in mind?"

Evelyn rose gracefully and fetched another music book. "Whenever we travel, we sometimes get to attend an opera. After I go, I buy the music and play it over and over. This is one of my favorite arias, from *Aïda*—when Aïda is so torn between her homeland, her father—and the man she loves."

Graced stared mutely as Evelyn shooed Daniel from the piano bench. She knew the story all too well. It was of Aïda, the Ethiopian slave of Amneris, daughter of the king of Egypt. She falls in love with Radames, captain of the Ethiopian guard, even though he is an enemy to her people and her mistress is set to marry him. Maybe Grace had always loved the story so much because of the way Aïda's father comes to rescue her—her father, the king of Ethiopia.

Martha sat up straight and said, "Grace, you should not. The very role we're hoping for this fall, the very song you—you—" "Botched in front of the most important people in New York's world of opera?" she finished faintly. She looked at Martha and added *for* her, "Including the Vanderbilts."

"Oh, my dear, I didn't know," Evelyn said.

Martha continued to address Grace. "You're not ready. You're on strict orders to not tax your voice."

With that Evelyn moved to close her book, but Grace stayed her hand. "No, please, I *want* to. Wasn't I saying earlier how your mountain air has been working wonders on me?" She smiled weakly. She might as well face this sooner rather than later. Maybe if she could sing this aria here, in front of the most favorable crowd possible, she could put the awful memory to rest. She turned from her aunt, who was wringing her hands, to Evelyn Monroe, who looked askance at her. Grace nodded.

As the dramatic, tumbling piano notes began, she remembered that day in late spring. Her father had sent the invitation to a rare dinner at his home, along with a note. "This will be a gathering of opera supporters. Be prepared to sing. Go to Watkins and get a new dress. Spare no expense. Charge to my account."

She had done so, and the golden creation she had purchased had helped lend her confidence, even when her father's son and his Worth-clad wife had coldly ignored her, and her half-sister had snuck curious glances at her as if she were a circus performer. She could never have told her father ahead of time that Monsieur LeMonte's intensified lessons, her aunt's pushing, and most especially her father's own expectations—which he suddenly had begun expressing—had been causing her sleepless nights and difficulties singing. They all expected her to show herself worthy. And what didn't she have to justify? Her father's money, her mother's life, Martha's wasted years, even her own existence. At least that was what gnawed inside her.

During dinner a debate had arisen between Anton Seidl and several of the other men. Hungarian Seidl, personal friend to Richard

Wagner, was the new music director for the Met. They contended whether *Aïda* was more Wagnerian or Verdian in form, and should be performed in its original Italian, or in German.

"Well, let's just hear it both ways, and then we can decide...if Miss Galveston will humor us." Seidl, and then all at the long, elaborate table, had turned to her.

But of course she would. This was her chance, her moment. It was as good as an audition. Yet more trepidation than excitement had filled her when she had stood in her father's parlor, ready to sing. She had not been able to get her breathing right. The faces had spun around her, her aunt's pinched, her father's imperious. She had recalled the few times her father had visited her as a child, how she had been dressed up and paraded, yet always too nervous to connect with the aloof man. It had been like that then, only far more awful, for it was public. Her voice had been stiff, shallow, and when she had cracked a high note she could no longer bear to look at him.

"I'm—I think I need to sit down," she had said at the end.

There had been no German version that night.

And now, Grace felt she had the opportunity to turn a corner, inspired by these wonderful people who surrounded her. Her voice was clear and pure as she began. *"Ritorna vicitor! E dal mio labbro uscì l'empia parola!"*

Her audience was motionless. She closed her eyes, remembering why she had once enjoyed singing, letting the music and emotions swirl around her, building. Evelyn's fingers created beautiful trills interspersed with heavy chords. As the aria culminated with the hauntingly beautiful *"Numi, pietà"* passage—"Gods, have pity on my suffering! There is no hope in my woe. Fatal love, tremendous love, break my heart or let me die!"—Grace knew she could not have given a better performance.

The room fell silent. Totally silent. She looked around for an expression, a word. They were merely staring at her. Amelia's hand was over her heart.

Then, from the next room where Melanie had been laid when she had fallen asleep, they heard a tiny cry. "Mommy?"

Grace's impassioned aria had awakened the child. Everyone burst into laughter. Emily Anne scurried out to get her daughter. "Oh, dear," Grace said, covering her cheek with her hand. "My dear, I'm afraid you have us quite speechless," Evelyn said. "Never have our walls been privy to such incredible music." "You are a prodigious talent." Judge Taylor stepped forward to bow gallantly over Grace's hand. "Thank you." Even as she accepted the compliment, she couldn't help herself; she glanced at Daniel.

He shook his head and repeated quietly, "A star."

Grace took a deep breath, feeling suddenly tired...but happy.

Emily Anne noticed the gesture as she re-entered holding Melanie. "Daniel, you should take Miss Galveston out to get some fresh air."

Daniel rose, but a rumpled head popped up from his sister's arms. "Uncle Danny!"

Clearly torn, not wanting to hurt the child, Daniel looked back and forth. Emily Anne settled the issue by announcing firmly that "Uncle Danny" had to be a nice host and Melanie could see him the next day. Daniel kissed his niece and offered his arm to Grace, escorting her into the garden. The sweet fragrance of roses and the nighttime humidity closed around them.

Grace turned to her companion. "I did it, just like at Lover's Leap!" she exclaimed. "You must be my good luck charm!"

"Are you ready to take me with you and return to New York?"

She laughed, then said seriously, "No. I don't want to go back yet. You can't imagine how horrible it was the last time I sang that aria. Worst of all...disappointing my father." Her voice, and face, fell.

Daniel put a finger under her chin to lift it. "It seems your father expects much but gives little."

"He doesn't view our financial support as little." Her eyes sought his.

Daniel's mouth tightened. "I'm not speaking of money. A child's physical needs should be met as a matter of course, lovingly, not as a begrudged duty, or in proportion to the child's performance. And as to emotional needs..."

"I've learned not to expect the impossible. My father just isn't like that." Her voice was small.

"Mine is."

"I know. I see—" She gestured to the home, with its lights gleaming within. "Your family is wonderful, gracious."

"I meant, my Heavenly Father. And yours." He studied her intently. "Or do you think God is as distant as your own father?"

"I—" Grace could not meet his gaze. Instead of answering, she whispered a confession, hoping to turn the conversation away from the uncomfortable subject of God. "I left him a message at our house, before we came here, you know. Telling him where we were. All he has to do is inquire with our footman, who has the address of The Cliff House. I keep checking for a letter or a telegram, but…"

"None come," Daniel finished for her.

"He won't come, either. It's idealistic of me, I know, hoping he might just show up, like Aïda's father—come to redeem me." She laughed lightly.

Grace was startled when Daniel's large hand gently cradled the side of her face. He was near, and his touch awakened all her senses. She sought his eyes, yearning, as usual, for the gentleness, the understanding she always found there. She leaned into his hand. His face, his lips, looked finely chiseled in the moonlight. Grace trembled, thinking he might kiss her.

But then his expression changed, as if a thought had just come to him. "Only God can redeem us. Do you know what I mean, Grace?"

The use of her given name softened his spiritual turn of mind only a little. She drew back ever so slightly, and he dropped his hand. "Why, yes," she said. After all, she went to church all the time, and hadn't Maum Sally drummed the love of Jesus into her all during her childhood?

Daniel smiled. He looked a little relieved. "I'm just afraid there's hurt you're carrying around inside you…that you don't have to. The Lord 'relieveth the fatherless and widow.' Whatever hole your father has left in your heart, Jesus can fill."

"You sound like Maum Sally," Grace said, then choked on a

completely unexpected lump of tears.

"Your mother's mammy?"

Wordlessly Grace nodded. What was he doing to her, gently unwrapping all her protective layers? She felt another one peel away as, sensing her emotion, he pulled her into his arms and laid his chin on top of her head. Her hands were trapped against his chest, and she could hear his heart beating beneath her ear. Her own was going much too fast for a comforting hug.

"She talked a lot about God?"

Again Grace nodded. Never had she felt more secure, but she was so awash in confusing feelings that she covered her face with her hands to withhold tears. Unfortunately that caused Daniel to release her and search for a handkerchief. She covered her face with it, exclaiming, "I'm just a mess!" as he patiently waited.

"Maybe some sleep will help," Daniel suggested.

She allowed him to lead her to the foot of the stairs in the entrance hall. Quiet voices still carried from the parlor.

"I'll make your excuses."

"Thank you."

She waited uncertainly, but he did not release her hand. "Good night, my dear Grace." With those intent eyes fastened on her, he raised her fingers to his lips and slowly kissed them.

Half an hour later, Grace heard the bedroom door open as Amelia entered. Still looking out the window, she softly admitted aloud, "I'm falling in love with him."

"What?" Amelia gasped. Quickly she shut the door.

Grace turned, her long white nightgown swirling around her bare feet. "It's true, I am. What do you think of that?"

Amelia stared a moment, then gave a sudden deep chortle. "I think Alice Hargrove will soon be sinking her claws into you. She's had her eye on Daniel since before I can remember."

"Has he...does he care for her, or someone else, perhaps?"

Amelia shrugged. "Lots of girls set their caps for him, but he's never responded. It's like he's...waiting."

"What about you, Amelia?"

"Me? What about me?"

"Yes," Grace said. "You and Daniel would surely be a perfect match. You have so much in common."

Amelia ignored her comment and instead pressed her with, "What will you do if he turns out to care for you in return? Would you actually stay here?"

"I don't know. I don't know! It's crazy—and I don't have any answers, only feelings—and who knows if it's not all just in my mind, anyway. But wait…you never answered *my* question." Grace fixed her friend with a suspicious stare.

Amelia came and sat nearby on the bed. She sighed. "Well, I'd be lying if I said Daniel didn't turn my head, or there weren't periods of time in the past when I had a crush on him. But that's all it ever was, just daydreams. And I can tell you, it's not all in your head. Daniel's never looked at me, or anyone, the way he looks at you."

Chapter Six

"You're going *where*?"

"To see Aunt Fannie, the famous hostess of Sinking Mountain."

Grace placed her second most plain dress in a valise along with her personal effects. She was wearing her plainest dress, having left off her bustle frame underskirt, and her hair was tied into a simple knot.

"Don't worry, Aunt, they've been there many times, and it will only be for a night or two."

"And you're traveling seven miles on bumpy back roads in a wagon—to arrive uninvited at the house of a woman you've never even seen?" Martha looked at her as if she were losing her mind.

"It's not unusual, Aunt Martha. Parties from Tallulah go there all the time. They say the food and hospitality are worth the ride, and Aunt Fannie wants the company to come. Amelia says she had 11 children—10 daughters!—and as they've grown up and married she's trained local girls to help serve all the visitors."

"She must have a large house."

"Actually, a log cabin."

Finally Martha put her foot down. "Are you crazy? What would make you want to do this? I think it's time I step in and forbid such foolishness."

Forbid? Grace had not thought it would come to that. She put on her most winsome expression. "But Aunt, it's growing so crowded here, with Professor Leon's walk happening at the end of the week. Some of my new friends decided it was the perfect time to enjoy the peace and quiet of the country, and I want to spend time with them. Next month we're going home. We'll be back plenty early to see Professor Leon cross the gorge. And meanwhile, Professor Schmidt and Mrs. Wylie want to take you to tea at Pine Terrace with the Mosses—and to dinner at the Wylie's! You'll hardly be alone."

Martha looked somewhat placated at the mention of the professor, who had continued to ply her with attention. She had also taken a liking to Mrs. Moss; their hostess was a sensible, gracious lady near Martha's own age with gentle dark eyes and a sweet smile. "Well..."

"If you still have doubts you could speak with the professor. He could reassure you this is a perfectly legitimate adventure."

"You've been spending an awful lot of time with that reverend."

"I've hardly seen him in three days!" Which, Grace thought, was the main reason she was so eager to set out this morning, though she would hardly say so to Martha. "Besides, you liked his family."

"They're quality people, I admit, but have you given no thought to Blake Greene?"

Grace paused. In fact, she hadn't. Her mind had been filled with Daniel Monroe. Yesterday she and Amelia had stood at the gorge rim and watched Professor Leon swim across the river far below. He had in his grasp the rope he would walk from Inspiration Point, one of the highest outcroppings, to Lover's Leap, on July 24. An intricate network of support ropes was being placed to secure the main line. Amelia had commented on the increased crowds.

"Alice has been stewing ever since Daniel invited you to Crown Pointe," she had told Grace. "She's using the number of people around here as an excuse to get up an outing to Aunt Fannie's. She figures at best you won't go because the trip is so arduous, giving her time alone with Daniel—and at worst, you will go, and she'll be able to make you look bad by demonstrating how poorly you endure hardship."

"Of all the nerve," Grace had huffed. And obviously, her mind had been made up. "But why is Daniel going? It seems like this would be a prime opportunity for him to mix with the people—you know, be an influence, invite them to church…"

Amelia had nodded. "Yes, that's why we've seen little of him these past days. But Alice knows he has a weak spot for visits to Mrs. Smith's, and it's been ages since we've gone. Mrs. Smith is a Baptist, but she and Daniel have great appreciation for one another."

"You ought to think of Blake Greene," said Aunt Martha firmly, drawing Grace's mind back to the present. "When you next see him, after this separation, I have little doubt that he'll be ready to speak of very serious matters. If you go—if I agree—you must consider *that* on your visit to the country."

"I will, Aunt Martha."

Martha sighed. "Very well, be off with you. And if you don't return *at least* by day after tomorrow, I'm sending a search party out after you."

Grace laughed, confident she was in safe hands. She kissed her aunt's cheek. "Why don't you come down and wave us off? No doubt Professor Schmidt is reading his newspaper in our lobby."

She enjoyed seeing straight-laced Martha grow flustered. But her aunt rose and followed her downstairs. There the said gentleman greeted them effusively, as predicted. Outside, the same group that had set off fireworks together on The Fourth of July was waiting for Grace. Trent slung her bag into the rear of a wagon and handed her up, for Alice had already positioned herself on the bench next to Daniel, who held the reins. Daniel called to the mules, and they were off.

They crossed Young's metal bridge. Soon the road ran by the river, which would have made the journey pleasant had it not been so bumpy. The surface deteriorated more the farther they went from town. Alice dominated the conversation. She spoke of local people and places of which Grace knew nothing. Grace determined to maintain a pleasant spirit and watched the scenery, which included the occasional farm. The houses generally were one-room affairs shingled with cedar or oak. There was often a spring house, a pig or chicken pen, and a barn or shed. She spied gardens burgeoning with tomatoes, beans and ripening pumpkins, sometimes staked out with what Amelia told her was a horizontally-hung bottle gourd, which was said to attract purple martins. The martins ate mosquitoes and helped keep crows from the nearby fields, where crops ripened in the summer sun, stalks of corn shooting up in neat rows.

At one house a woman waved to them as they passed. She was stretching threads between two racks. There was a break in the conversation, so Grace asked, "What is she doing?"

Alice gave a laugh. "How do you think these people get their clothes? They don't order them from a tailor like you do."

Daniel frowned at her. He explained to Grace, "She's using the warping bars to prepare the threads so they can be ready for weaving on the loom. That's what's done with flax or cotton or sheep's wool—after it's combed and carded."

"And spun. See the wheel on the porch?" Amelia added, pointing. "Some of the women still produce their own dyes from local plants. Pokeweed berries for rose, bloodroot for red, indigo for blue, walnut hulls for brown."

"Oh," said Grace, amazed at Amelia's knowledge. Though she had known country people made their own clothing, she could not imagine so much time being devoted to their creation.

"The original land lots in this area were of 202 ½ acres," Daniel told her informatively. "The people work very hard simply to exist. They learned much from the Cherokees. They burn off sections of their land to plant crops, then after a few years use the area for grazing, then let it go back to forest while planting new acreage. That system is best on the land. So many of the trees are already being stripped away by the railroads and the copper mines and fed to these new steam-powered sawmills. But I must say, growing produce for the hotels has helped supplement the incomes of some families. Fannie Smith's farm is one of the largest and most profitable. She's really turned her talent in the kitchen into an industry."

"I hope she has fried chicken for supper," Amelia commented.

"I could stand some now," Trent said.

Daniel nodded to a clearing by the river. "I can pull over there for us to have a short lunch break."

They all voiced their enthusiasm. Minutes later they were devouring the sandwiches, apples and cheese Mrs. Wylie had graciously packed into a hamper. The mules had a long drink of the river water. When the time came to move on, Grace was loath to get back into the wagon.

Daniel seemed to sense her quandary, for he suggested, "Would you like to walk with me a while? You and Amelia? I know you've taken quite a beating in the back."

"I'd love to," Grace responded quickly. She ignored Alice's cold stare.

Trent drove the mules with Alice at his side. The other three walked ahead to avoid the dust stirred by the wheels. Grace felt much better with some food in her stomach and stretching her aching limbs rather than having to brace herself against the jostling wagon. And of course it was better with Alice behind them, even glowering as she was, rather than at Daniel's side!

Daniel chuckled. "I've got to tell you a story," he said suddenly. "About Aunt Fannie."

Grace turned an attentive smile on him.

"Tourists used to trade with the Cherokee in these parts. But in the winter, the Indians had it rough. The last of the tribesmen of Chief Gray Eagle would sometimes camp on the Smith property during cold weather. Aunt Fannie would feed them. Many times she invited them to church. She worked on the chief a long time, and at last he consented to go with her. So they went down to Wolf Creek Baptist. The preacher started off quiet, but then he got going, as Baptists are sometimes apt to do." Daniel paused to chuckle good-naturedly. "He was gesturing wildly and loudly describing the pits of hell. Chief Gray Eagle had never seen a white man carry on like that. He stood up and declared 'Whiskey too much. Whiskey too much.'"

Everyone laughed, though Grace guessed the others had heard the tale many times. "What happened then?" she asked.

"The chief left, never to return."

"Now if he'd come to an Episcopal church, he surely would have been saved," Amelia declared jokingly.

More laughter. Suddenly Daniel yelled, "Grace!" and nearly lifted her off her feet, drawing her back against him. When she saw the reason, she stumbled and grabbed him. Trent quickly stopped the mules and backed them up.

"Easy, it's all right," Daniel whispered in her ear, pulling both Grace and Amelia slowly back from the six-foot-long rattlesnake that had been sunning itself on the road.

Grace covered her mouth, horrified that she had almost treaded mere inches from the snake's head. Out of the corner of her eye she had thought it a stick. Disturbed by all the commotion, the creature slithered silently into the grass near the riverbank.

"I—I think I'll ride again," she said.

"I'm sorry…I should've been watching. We see a snake almost every time."

"I'll definitely ride again." Grace clamored into the back of the wagon, not waiting for assistance. As she sat down, she didn't miss the smug smile on Alice's face.

By the time they arrived on the Smith property, Grace was sweaty, sore and miserable. She surveyed the farm, eager for refreshment. A smaller structure joined the large 1840s cabin by a covered porch. A high board fence just in front of the stacked stone chimney enclosed a lush garden, where Grace saw tall green plants clustered thickly together. A woman clad in black came out onto the porch, where several other people already lounged, chatting and sipping lemonade. Clearly they were not Aunt Fannie's only visitors.

"Why, it's Rev. Monroe and his town friends," exclaimed the hostess, stepping down and smiling broadly. Grace judged her to be about 60, with her graying dark hair parted in the middle and drawn back into a bun.

Daniel hopped down from the wagon and bounded over to kiss her hand. "Aunt Fannie, it's been far too long. No one in town can hold up a debate on religion and politics quite like you."

"Oh, nonsense," she said and swatted him, laughing. "How long are you come for?"

"A night or two, if you've room."

"I've always room."

"And fried chicken?" Amelia inquired as she climbed out of the wagon.

"That, too, Miss Wylie." Fannie Smith turned a welcoming smile on the girl.

"I've brought someone new," Daniel added, and drew Grace forward to be introduced. The little lady's dark eyes, hooded but sparkling, fell upon her. "Miss Grace Galveston, from New York City."

After Grace had curtsied and Fannie bowed her head in acknowledgement, Fannie said, "I had someone from there last week, an architect. Right now there are three from Athens. Students from the university."

The gentlemen on the porch took their cue, rising to meet them. The Thomas brothers, John and Simon, greeted them with great charm and manners, communicated in the warm drawl of Southern gentlemen. The third guest, Richard Carraway, was a slender, quiet young man with a passion for botany. Apparently this interest was the main reason for their visit to Tallulah, and kept the young man often in the woods.

They took their bags to their rooms. It was dark inside the cabin even with the shutters open. Grace was shown to a rope bed covered with a beautiful handmade quilt that she would share with Amelia. Alice would be on a trundle bed that pulled out below. Long accustomed to having not only her own bed but also her own room, Grace wondered how she would fare sleeping. She doubted that even the cluster of ribbon-tied lavender Fannie had left on their pillows would help on that score.

Grace, however, didn't even let out a sigh while Alice was within earshot. She noticed there was a little table with an oil lamp perched on a doily to one side of the bed, and a trunk at the foot. The girls took turns putting away their things and washing the dust away at the basin, using scented lye soap and embroidered hand towels, before venturing into the main part of the house.

Fannie was busy overseeing the preparation of dinner, and Daniel and Trent had engaged the students in a discussion, so the ladies decided to stroll over the property. A man was working in a field among crops laid out in neat rows. Mr. Smith, Grace guessed. As the sun drifted down, igniting a red-orange glow on the horizon, crickets chirped in the thickets. They passed an orchard.

"Apples?" asked Grace.

Amelia nodded. "They do very well here. Settlers used to move around so frequently that they didn't take time to cultivate apple trees. It's really due to the Cherokees and Jarvis Van Buren—the same one who built in Clarkesville—that we have the trees around here that we do now."

"What did Mr. Van Buren do?"

"He founded the Georgia Pomological Society in the 1850s and convinced people growing apples would be profitable."

"He also collected mountain varieties and named them," Alice, who trailed along behind them, added.

"Oh, you should taste our own Mountaine Belle!" Amelia exclaimed with delight, rolling her eyes as if she imagined the crunch and the juice on her tongue at that very moment. "There's nothing like a crisp apple on a fall day, with the trees all orange and gold. The farmers have cornshuckings, where all the harvested corn is brought into the barn or a cleared field. Everyone divides into teams to see who can shuck their pile first. Sometimes a red ear is hidden in one pile, and whoever finds it gets a prize. It's all a big party, with lots of food and dancing."

"But of course Grace won't be here then, which is just as well, since she'd surely find such an activity quite primitive," Alice commented.

Grace chose to ignore her. "It is beautiful here now," Grace admitted. "It's hard to think it could get any prettier."

"Tomorrow we'll take you to Sinking Mountain," Amelia said.

"Yes, I've been wondering about that."

Alice spoke up again. "After today's travel, the hike might be a bit too much for Miss Galveston. We have to remember, Amelia, she's not accustomed to our terrain."

"Nonsense. It's just a short walk."

"Why is it called 'sinking'?" Grace asked her.

"The ground really is soft. In certain spots, it feels like it's giving way beneath your feet."

Alice added, "The early settlers decided the Cherokee were right—that the Yunwi Tsundi had a large mining operation going on under the mountain." She pushed her way between the other two and turned to Grace with feigned concern, the sun glowing on her golden hair. Unfortunately, she really was pretty, Grace thought. "Truly, Miss Galveston, if you decide you need to rest, no one would think the less of you. Some say the view is not very remarkable."

"I'm sure I'll be fine," Grace replied stiffly. "It's hardly as if my health is failing."

"The mountain may not look like much at a glance, but the view off the eastern side is wonderful, in *my* opinion," Amelia rejoined. "There's a breath-taking plunge down to the Chattooga River. I believe you'd find it worth the walk."

"It's settled, then." Grace linked her arm through Amelia's, effectively nudging Alice ahead of them. Amelia gave Grace a conspiratorial smirk.

They returned to the cabin for a meal that justified all the day's hardships. Grace thought she had never tasted more delicious chicken, garden vegetables and fluffy biscuits with fresh honey. After dinner one of the students produced a guitar, and they gathered on the porch to enjoy the music floating away into the still night. The ladies helped Aunt Fannie string fresh beans from the garden so that they could be hung to dry, to help feed visitors that would come when the weather was cool and the garden not so verdant. There were no horse hooves, no train whistles, no raucous voices…just perfect tranquility.

* * *

The following day after breakfast, they took the trail to Sinking Mountain. The students decided to accompany them. The pace was not vigorous at all, for the budding botanist kept stopping to exclaim over the flora and fauna and collect samples into a multi-compartmented box. At one point he pointed and exclaimed with great delight, "Ah, ginseng! See, those plants that look almost like tiny human figures?"

Amelia bent low for a look as Richard pushed back the summer underbrush and decaying leaves. "Yes, it's supposed to have numerous health benefits," she said. She grinned at him in a flash of understanding. "Rather like a treasure hunt, isn't it?"

Richard nodded and returned her smile. "Exactly. This ginseng is not unlike the Chinese variety. It takes years to mature."

"And brings seng hunters a good price at market."

"Aunt Fannie told me that, even years ago, the Cherokee medicine people were said to pass by three stalks before harvesting the fourth."

As Richard squatted and opened his box, Alice, obviously bored with the exchange, commented, "Apparently no such compunction has overtaken *you*."

"It's not as though I'm harvesting an immature specimen, *one* specimen," the botany student muttered under his breath. Alice easily ignored him and Amelia's glare, as well.

The others chuckled to lighten the moment and moved ahead over the next rise. They startled some deer and enjoyed the sight of white tails bobbing as the creatures bounded gracefully down the slope. While they waited for Richard to join them again, Daniel told them about the foxes, coyotes, bobcats and black bears that made their home in the mountains.

Alice was quiet for the rest of the outing, but Grace could sense her growing irritation as Daniel stayed by Grace's side, sharing interesting facts and offering his hand to help her over fallen trees and jutting roots. When they reached their destination, he sat with her looking over the Chattooga River Valley, eating the lunch Aunt Fannie had prepared. By the time they again neared the Smith property, the tension was almost palpable.

As they sat down to a supper of ham, greens, cornbread, beans and stewed apples, Alice finally broke her cold silence. "You must find all this quite tedious, Miss Galveston."

"Tedious? Why?" Grace glanced not at Alice, but at Aunt Fannie, who pretended not to notice as she placed a pitcher of iced tea on the table.

"You're used to such sophisticated amusements in New York."

"I think everyone knows I came here seeking peace, not amusement."

"And why was that? Don't most notable New Yorkers go to Newport for the summer?"

"Well, yes, but it's hardly a rule."

Everyone chuckled.

"Miss Galveston is an opera singer," Alice told the group from Athens. "Maybe we can coax her to sing for our entertainment tonight."

The men murmured in agreement, but Amelia protested, "There's nothing like putting her on the spot."

"Well, Mr. Thomas played his guitar last night. *He* wasn't shy. Surely if Miss Galveston can sing for the Vanderbilts our little group wouldn't make her nervous." Alice paused with her fork in midair, pretending to think. "Oh, dear, that's right. Someone said—maybe it was you, Amelia—that there was something about an embarrassing incident before you came? Something about needing to rest your voice, Grace, so you can be ready to return to the stage this fall?" Alice turned her questioning catty eyes on Grace, whose color deepened. She was too taken aback at the girl's temerity to reply.

"It wasn't me!" Amelia declared. "I don't know where you heard that!"

"Oh. Maybe it was from Daniel, then. I mean, *Rev.* Monroe."

"Hardly." Daniel stiffened in his chair. "Really, Miss Hargrove, this is too much. I can tell you that Miss Galveston sang most beautifully, and perfectly, while visiting with us at my parents' home."

Grace smiled at him while Alice's mouth firmed at the reminder, and the rebuke.

John Thomas, the most outgoing and gallant of the students, responded to the awkwardness of the situation by chiming in, "Actually, instead of making you all listen to my inexpert strumming again, I was hoping Miss Wylie would join me for a game of checkers tonight."

Amelia looked up in complete surprise. "Me?"

"I do love a good game of checkers, and I hear the same of you."

"Oh, yes—I'd love to!" She didn't notice Richard Carraway's suddenly downcast expression.

As they rose from dinner, Daniel volunteered to assist Aunt Fannie in clearing the table. She took him up on his offer but shooed away all other attempts to help. Alice was watching Grace. Grace had expected Alice to retreat in the face of her companions' disapproval. Instead, the girl's growing resentment would apparently not let her rest...or Grace, either.

"It's because he'll talk politics with her," Alice said as they left the table. "Aunt Fannie always campaigns all over the county for her candidates, and has her family do the same. Daniel will be a while. What will you do?"

"I'm sure I'll find something," Grace replied. She started to move away from Alice, but then realized that honestly, she *didn't* know where to go!

Her moment of hesitation was enough to prompt Alice to continue. In a voice filled with false sympathy she said: "You must feel just like a fish out of water, being out here in the absolute *wilderness*. In town during the tourist season, that's one thing. But when the people leave, even Tallulah is really quite small-town. Almost as quiet as it is, well, right now. You must be looking forward to returning to New York."

"Not really."

"But surely you'll have to go back and take up your singing soon. I'm sure once you get swept up in all the glamour of that scene, all this will probably seem like a dream." She laughed carelessly. "Like you've never even been here."

"You'd like that, wouldn't you, Alice?" Grace snapped, her

patience gone at last. Not waiting for a reaction, she turned on her heel and marched across the room and onto the front porch, where Mr. Thomas and Amelia were setting up for their game. Mr. Carraway perched on the top step and scratched with a fountain pen in a small notebook. They all looked up as she stomped past.

"Where are you going?" Amelia asked.

"For a walk. I need some fresh air," Grace tossed over her shoulder.

"Do you want me to go with you?" Faintly. Not enthusiastic.

"No, that's all right."

"Well, it's almost dark. Don't be gone long."

"I won't go far."

But as she walked it felt good, and she found herself on the trail to Sinking Mountain that they had taken earlier in the day. *It's not like I can get lost going this same way*, she told herself.

Why had she let Alice's silly comments stir her up so? Maybe because while the girl's tactics were childish, her words did contain some truth. Grace soon would have to return to New York. The thought made her feel empty. She wanted to sing, she *did*. But not to gain her father's admiration. She would just have to settle it in her mind once and for all that Hampton Galveston's opinion had no bearing on her career.

She sighed, knowing that not caring about what her father thought would be just as impossible as not wanting to see the affection in Daniel Monroe's eyes. And what could come of that? They could write, of course, and she could vacation here again next summer. But what might happen between now and then, over the course of a whole year? She would have to answer Blake Greene's expected question of matrimony, and Daniel might notice what a gem had always been right here beneath his nose…Amelia.

As a whip-o-will sounded a mournful note, Grace stopped. She had been so involved in her inner ramblings that she had failed to notice the sun dropping below the horizon. The soft curve of the hills was a darkening silhouette. She had better go back.

Retracing her steps, she had not gone far when she realized

nothing looked familiar. She came to a fork in the path that she hadn't noticed passing earlier. Well, it had to be the one that led downhill, not the trail continuing around the mountain. She must have gone farther and faster than she had intended to.

After walking several more minutes without the Smith farm coming into view, Grace's heart began to beat fast, faster than the exertion of her exercise called for. It was impossible! She could *not* have gotten lost on such a short walk!

Dark was falling. There was nothing to do but continue. After a few minutes, though, the path began to wind upwards. That was all wrong. Grace stopped and wrung her hands. Maybe if she were closer to the homestead than she thought, they would hear if she called out.

"Hello? Hello!"

Her voice rang back at her. Then the silence mocked.

Grace decided to go back the other way. As she turned quickly and strode ahead, her boot caught on an exposed root, sending her flying over the edge of the hillside. She grabbed for a sapling, but her momentum kept her going. She screamed as she tumbled headlong into a dense stand of mountain laurel. It closed around her like an evil curtain. She was sliding, sliding. The limbs plucked at her clothing and scraped her skin, and she covered her head to protect her face.

Then, she was motionless at last. Grace tried to push the branches away, but any attempt to move, to ascertain the way out, brought pain from the many claw-like thorns that grasped her. Hadn't Daniel told them about "laurel hells," places where the plants grew so thick they choked out all other growth and even the light? Hunting dogs and even sometimes people who became entangled had been known to never emerge. And now she was in the midst of one.

Grace fought back panic. They would come looking for her, she told herself. She just had to remain calm and try to get out into the opening so they could reach her. Keeping her face down as much as possible, she crawled slowly forward. Tears filled her eyes as thorns tore through her light-weight blouse and into her skin. A sob escaped her, and she was about to lie down in hopelessness when she noticed it was lighter to her left. Grace edged her way painstakingly in that direction.

Seemingly an eternity later, she was free!

The ground leveled out for a space before dropping again into a dark ravine. She huddled next to a tree on the flat surface. She had no idea which way to go. She simply must wait and hope the men would find her soon. Besides, she had twisted her ankle when she fell, and it ached now. Absently she rubbed it.

Grace heard a soft rustling on the forest floor. With a shudder, she thought of the rattler they had seen the day before. If one crept up on her, it was too dark now for her to know until it was too late. She was unaccustomed to such helplessness. So it seemed an appropriate time to do something unusual. Pray.

Grace's attempts to wing her requests heavenward were cut brutally short by a sound that turned her blood cold and raised the tiny hairs on the back of her neck. A sound she had never heard before. It was like a cry of the utmost suffering, a woman's dying scream. She guessed it must be a bobcat. And not too far away. The last bit of her composure gone, she covered her head with her arms, crying and trembling violently.

Chapter Seven

Daniel was drying dishes with a checked towel, giving Mrs. Smith his reflections on the performance of the current Tallulah Falls commissioners, when Amelia walked into the kitchen.

"You're still here?" she asked.

"Well, yes, there were a lot of dishes," he said with a lopsided grin. But her worried expression caused him to quickly add, "Why? Is something wrong?"

"If Grace isn't with you, Daniel, like I thought she was by now, I'm afraid something's *very* wrong."

Aunt Fannie turned from the sink to look at Amelia, and Daniel put down his cloth. He stepped toward her. "Tell me."

"She went out for a walk after dinner. Alice kept nettling her. I assumed she had surely returned by now. But I—didn't check." Tears filled her eyes. "I was too involved in my game."

"Tell the men," Fannie directed Amelia. "I'll fetch lanterns and guns."

As she hurried out, Daniel's gaze met Amelia's. They didn't need to say that Grace should have returned long ago…that anything could have happened. Daniel asked, "Which way did she go?"

Amelia shook her head. "I don't know. I'm sorry."

They began by combing the farm, yelling "Grace!" When no

reply resulted, Daniel was torn between taking the road into town or the trail towards Sinking Mountain. But the road had been rutted, whereas the path was smoother and more pleasant for walking. While the other men hiked off down the road, he and Trent took the trail, splitting up at the fork.

Daniel had not gone far after turning left when he was momentarily arrested by the cry of the bobcat. The gun he carried was loaded, and he was a good shot. He hurried on, imagining Grace lost and maybe hurt. The forest could be terrifying at night to a woman accustomed only to city life. He paused, lifted the lantern, and yelled, "Grace!"

No response. He continued, calling her name at regular intervals. Maybe the cat would slink away toward the river, discouraged by all the commotion. Bobcats were generally not aggressive unless provoked.

Then, at last—he thought he heard a voice!

"I'm here! Daniel, down here!"

He looked downhill from where he stood on the path and saw a form crumpled against a tree, not far from the edge of a sea of laurel and rhododendron. Grace! She rose slowly, leaning on the tree trunk for support.

"Are you all right?" he called.

"Scratched—I fell into the laurel—and terrified—"

Daniel was already sliding down the hill on the flats of his boots, holding up the gun in one hand and the lantern in the other. He was so relieved to see her, so filled with emotion, that he immediately set both at her feet, leaned in, cradled her face in his hands, and kissed her. Not gently. Intensely. Instantly her arms went around him and her soft lips parted beneath his. He didn't have to think, didn't *want* to think, because it was the very thing they had both been waiting on to happen. Daniel held nothing back. He had never kissed a woman like this, never.

Grace trembled in his arms and, turning her face downward, sagged against him as if her strength were suddenly gone. He dropped his arms to her waist, holding her up.

"Should I apologize?" he whispered.

"If you do I'll never forgive you. Thank you for coming for me." But then in the dim light he noticed the scratches on her face. He touched one and his finger came away wet. "You're bleeding!" he exclaimed.

"The laurel. I was so afraid I'd never get out of it!"

"And your clothes are torn!" he exclaimed as his gaze dropped and with horror he took in the ripped white fabric, already darkened with blood. Quickly he shrugged out of his vest and carefully slipped her arms through the holes. "I'm sorry. What a cad I was to not even notice, to just grab you like that!"

"No!" she exclaimed very firmly. Grace touched his face. "I'm so glad—so glad you came."

Her voice choked on a sob, and he kissed her again. Gingerly she stepped in close, seeming to need his nearness. Her body fit so neatly against his. He had only ever imagined such magic. He wanted to love and protect this woman forever. Then guilt overcame passion, and he drew back, saying, "We should get you back, let Aunt Fannie look at those cuts."

"*Scratches.*"

"Yeah, right. Let's go."

Grace took a few steps and stopped. She shook her head as Daniel looked questioningly at her. "I'm afraid it's going to take me a while, and I'm going to need your arm to lean on. My ankle—it twisted when I fell. It's not bad. I can walk, if you'll be patient with me."

"Nonsense." Daniel slung the strap of the gun across his back and handed Grace the softly glowing lantern. Then, despite her gasp of surprise, he placed one arm gently under her back and a hand under her knees, and picked her up.

"I'm sorry," he said as she winced in pain. Carefully he headed up the hill, back to the path.

"Daniel, this is very gallant, but you're a preacher, not a lumberjack. No one would expect you to carry me all the way back."

"I can do it. You're light as a feather."

"Say that again in five minutes."

He puffed a laugh. "So long as I don't have to carry on a conversation, I can do it," he repeated.

With that, Grace laid her head against his shoulder and was as still as a little girl. He did feel rather like a conquering knight. When they met up with Trent, he refused assistance even though he was growing winded. He carried Grace into the cabin, ignoring Alice's wide-eyed stare and Amelia's clamoring.

Once Grace was tenderly deposited on the bed, Fannie set to work washing the blood from her face. Daniel told her of the hurt ankle.

"Elevate it, and I'll prepare a poultice."

She called for her granddaughter to help her make a healing salve for the scratches. The girl went into the garden after aloe while Fannie unwrapped herbs from paper packets.

Amelia sat beside Grace and started to unlace her boots, saying, "Grace, I'm so sorry. I should have gone with you. It's all my fault."

"It certainly was not. And really, I can unlace my own boot."

They both stopped and looked at him. "You'll have to go," they said in unison, which would have caused him to laugh had he been less concerned.

Fannie turned from her work to behold Daniel's blank expression. "She'll be fine," the woman urged. "But I have to tend those cuts. You've done your part. Now go."

Daniel remembered the torn bodice under his vest that Grace wore and quickly rose. "I'll be back later," he assured Grace.

"You'll see her in the morning," Fannie told him gently but firmly.

"But Mrs. Smith—"

"In the morning." Greater firmness.

Knowing when he was defeated, Daniel decided to retreat. But not before he bent and, in front of watching eyes, gently kissed Grace's forehead.

"Thank you," she said softly again.

As he closed the door behind him, he heard Fannie Smith say, "My, but our reverend is a goner."

* * *

Daniel was uncharacteristically cranky the next day. He knew Trent would have driven the wagon, allowing him to ride in the back with Grace, who had been positioned as comfortably as possible with her foot up on a valise. He knew that was what she wanted. But he had chosen to drive. At least maybe his silence would finally give Alice the message that she did not interest him.

Women had always swooned over his appearance. But his mother had taught him that true beauty came from within. Thus, he had handled feminine attentions with both courtesy and modesty. For the truly determined, he had simply administered the perfect test by disclosing his occupation. That usually weeded them out pretty quickly.

Grace had been different. She seemed drawn to him on all levels, not at all discouraged by his strong spiritual foundation. In fact, she seemed to seek out his Christian qualities. But was that because she shared them, or she needed them?

He frowned. He had let himself drift along, being drawn into a relationship, without having a clear sense of her Christian commitment. He had let her surface comments satisfy him. Daniel was well aware that differences between them in this area could prove a far greater obstacle than mere geography.

He felt her studying him, sensed her wondering at this change in his demeanor. He turned and smiled his assurance, the sight of her wide brown eyes melting him to his core. "Doing all right?" he asked. "Need a break?"

"I'm fine."

Daniel returned to his reverie, rubbing his two-day growth of beard with one hand. He must look a sight. Not only was he unshaven, and sorely in need of a good bath, but his eyes were probably bloodshot, too. He had not slept well last night. The thoughts he had had while kissing her had kept running through his mind: *to love and protect*. The phrase came straight from the vows of holy matrimony, for heaven's sake! Was he really in love with Grace Galveston? They must have a talk, and soon.

He spent the rest of the journey conversing silently and intently with God about this woman who was driving him crazy.

They pulled up in front of the hotel. Daniel jumped down and walked around to the rear of the wagon, just as Amelia helped Grace swing her legs down. With a crooked smile he asked, "Shall I carry you in, ma'am?"

"Let's not make a scene." Grace looked around at the throngs of people. It was far busier in town than was usual even for the summer. Until that moment, Daniel had forgotten about the aerialist.

"I think if we both take an arm she can manage," Amelia offered.

Daniel grabbed Grace's valise and did as instructed. In this manner they helped her into the lobby.

"What in the world—?"

Martha Hampton was already striding toward them, gaping in shock at her niece. Salve still shone on the scratches on Grace's fair skin. She wore the untorn dress she had originally set off with in her valise. While it at least covered the cuts on her torso, it was stained and wrinkled from the journey.

"This is the last time you go off into the wilderness, the *last time*!" Martha exclaimed, as if Grace were a wayward five-year-old.

"I'm fine, Aunt Martha. Mrs. Smith said you won't even be able to see the scratches in a few days, and my ankle was merely twisted, not sprained. Really I can walk just fine." And she shook off her assistants to demonstrate that fact.

By way of further explanation, Daniel told the older woman, "Miss Galveston went for a walk alone yesterday and fell down a slope into some laurel."

Grace shrugged lamely. "What's a wilderness adventure without getting lost at least once?" she said in an attempt to be lighthearted.

"*Lost?*" Martha was even more rattled. "Oh, good heavens! What were you people doing, letting her go off alone? Look at you. This is *not* what I had in mind for your reunion. What will Blake Greene think? I knew I was overriding my better judgment by letting you go off to this Fannie Mae's—"

"Fannie Smith's," corrected Amelia.

But Daniel was watching Grace, who had turned pale and repeated, "Blake Greene?"

"Yes, Blake Greene."

"He's here?"

"Yes, it was to be a surprise. I made his reservation when I made ours, after he told me that he would be able to take a break from his firm later in the summer."

Amelia looked confused. She had the naiveté to ask what Daniel found frozen in his throat. "What does this Blake Greene person have to do with anything?"

Martha turned to her, brows raised. "A great deal, once he finally speaks his mind—which I have no doubt he has come to do." She turned her sharp, withering gaze on Daniel.

Daniel felt like a thousand Chinese firecrackers were going off inside his head. He looked at Grace, whose lips trembled. And he had thought her so honest, so open! His voice came out like a growl. "Why didn't you tell me you had a fiancé?"

"He's not my fiancé!" Grace protested.

But the distress on her face clearly showed he was *something*.

At that moment a disbelieving masculine voice spoke from the stairs. "Grace?"

Daniel's eyes shifted to take in the tall, elegantly dressed young man standing on the steps. He had wheat-blonde hair, blue eyes, aristocratically proportioned features, and a muscular frame. His expression betrayed both joy and concern as it fastened on the object of his affection. Then he jogged down to meet her, bracing his hands on her arms and kissing her forehead.

"What has happened to you, my dear?"

Grace drew back, flustered. "I—Blake, this is Amelia Wylie, my friend, and—"

Daniel watched as Mr. Greene bowed chivalrously over Amelia's hand, then turned toward him. The man's hand came out. Daniel's hand, like his face, felt frozen. Not for all the good breeding in the world did he think he could make it leave his side. He felt Martha

86

Hampton smirking smugly at him, fully aware of his inward battle. Then he realized it wasn't Blake Greene's fault that the man's almost-fiancée had two-timed him. He forced himself to shake hands, just as Mr. Greene was about to give up on him. Grace was so uncertain about the exchange that apparently she had no further words of introduction.

"Rev. Daniel Monroe, Grace's other *friend*," Daniel found himself saying coldly. He looked at Grace, not bothering to hide his anger. Ignoring her hurt and pleading expression, he added, "Clearly, Miss Galveston is back in good hands, so I'll be taking my leave."

He didn't wait for anyone else to speak, but spun on his heel and marched away. Grace called to him in an anguished tone. He just let the door swing shut behind him.

Chapter Eight

Two days later, Grace was so desperate to talk with Daniel that her only notice of the commotion surrounding the feat scheduled for the aerialist J. A. St. John, son of the 1884 Prohibition Party presidential candidate, was impatience that the crowds made it all the less likely that she would be able to locate the young minister. Trains were said to be backed up for over a mile, bringing spectators from as far away as South Carolina, Florida and Alabama. The Tallulah Gorge walk had been billed as the highest and longest ever to be attempted. St. John would balance himself with a 46 pound, 30-foot-long pole as he crossed 1,440 feet across the chasm—with a drop of around 1,000 feet to the rushing waters below.

Amelia had graciously agreed to go a second time to Daniel's home and also to the church. On this occasion she took a note which she was to stick under the door should she find him again absent.

Daniel, please, we need to talk. If you are unable to come before, I will attend the ball tonight at the hotel. Grace Galveston.

"This is so not like him," Amelia told Grace when she joined her for tea at The Cliff House, having delivered the note to the residence but seen no trace of the occupant. "He's usually so calm and level-headed."

"Do you think he'll come tonight?"

Amelia shrugged, then said, "I have to think it doubtful. Daniel has nothing against dancing, but some of his older parishioners do, so he generally doesn't frequent the ballroom scene." She noticed Grace's woebegone expression. "But who knows. He has to face you sooner or later."

"Does he?"

"Unless he's totally taken leave of his senses, his personality will urge him to have things out in the open and settled. He's not the type to let people dangle. Perhaps he just needs to think through some things." Amelia took a sip of her tea. She put down the cup, fidgeted, cleared her throat. Then she continued rather cautiously. "Grace, you and I have not spoken much of spiritual matters. I wish now that we had. I'm not sure exactly where you stand, but I do know that any woman who might become Daniel's wife would—"

She stopped, looking over Grace's shoulder. She couldn't control a fleeting look of disappointment when she saw Blake Greene approaching.

He seemed oblivious to their previous conversation. "Odds are running even to 2-to-1 that Leon won't complete the walk," he said as he pulled out a chair and sat down.

Amelia recovered herself quickly. "*Won't* complete it?" she repeated. "Surely they don't think...?"

It was Blake's turn to shrug. He leaned back and crossed one leg over the other, popping a lemon tart into his mouth.

"You didn't bet, did you?" asked Grace.

Blake grinned. "My dear, with odds like that, what man could resist?"

Daniel would resist, thought Grace unexpectedly.

"I laid a neat bundle in *favor* of the daring gent. There's quite a scene out there...vendors selling food and drink...that Mr. Young selling souvenir photos of Leon...more people arriving by the minute. Folks are estimating more than 6,000 may come today. I'd suggest if you ladies are almost finished with tea, we might wish to secure our spots along the rim."

"We have to wait on Aunt Martha. She was still napping when we came down."

Blake frowned. "Should you go up and check on her? Someone could easily move the stools we set out this morning. Unfortunately, not everyone in attendance will share our code of conduct."

Grace sighed and rose to do as he suggested. Before turning away, she patted Amelia's arm. "We'll talk later," she promised.

Amelia looked up and smiled faintly. "All right. I must go meet my parents now anyway."

When the two women left the table, Blake sat back down to finish up the leftovers. He could hardly be termed doting, Grace thought as she mounted the hotel stairs. But at the same time he seemed quite confident of his claim on her. After Grace's initial vague explanation that Daniel was a new friend with whom she'd had a misunderstanding, Blake had seemed to wave off the incident in the lobby. He'd laughingly referred a few times since to "that mad minister." He didn't seem to notice how that made Grace bristle.

Half an hour later, on Blake's dandily proffered arm, Grace made her way through the throngs. Martha sailed grandly along at Blake's other side. In view of his height and imposing appearance, most people fell away in front of them. Ladies stared at him as much as men did at Grace. She knew they made a smart couple, well able to hold their own even strolling down Fifth Avenue. But today she felt shy, not wanting to be noticed. Her gait was quite normal and her scratches were almost healed, and were easily covered with a bit of facial powder, thanks to the medications Aunt Fannie had sent back with her. So maybe her reticence came more from the fact that so many people had recently seen her on Daniel's arm...or worse, that *he* might be anywhere in the crowd, watching her.

Grace took a seat on the stool they had brought and raised her parasol. Her eyes were fixed on the spider web of guy wires supporting the main rope which Leon would traverse. But her mind was on her personal dilemma.

Daniel had never spoken of love or marriage. Yet his actions— and his kiss—had told her much. And if he didn't care, why had he stormed off at the sight of Blake? If he were at the ball tonight, she would find a few private moments in which to explain that yes, Blake had been courting her in New York, but that she hadn't mentioned it because she had hardly thought of him since meeting Daniel. That would provide the perfect opening for them to discuss their feelings for one another. And if it came to that, what then? Like a tightrope walker, would she be willing to put everything on the line, do whatever she must, to have his love?

The crowd exploded into excited talk and cheering. Grace looked to the far side of the gorge, where a slender man with curling dark hair and moustache, and a body-fitting costume, was approaching Inspiration Point.

"There he is," Blake said, though the man carrying the huge pole was unmistakable.

Martha announced, "This is the craziest thing I have ever seen."

It was 5:20. Professor Leon stepped onto the rope and slowly, methodically, started forward. Grace looked at the faces of all the people jammed into every nook and cranny and lining the balconies of the nearby hotels. All of them in view were anxious and afraid, watching in tense silence.

It was indeed a rather awful thing, seeing the small figure balancing so perilously suspended above the maw of the earth, so vulnerable. Grace found herself holding her breath. How must the man's poor wife and four-year-old daughter feel, watching not far away? How must they feel *every* time Mr. St. John took such a risk? Surely the suspense must wear on them.

Then, the unthinkable happened. A loud snapping noise shot through the air. A collective gasp issued forth as the main line, upon which the professor stood not yet halfway over the gorge, began to sway dramatically. Grace rose, hand at her heart. People cried out. Leon made several exaggerated movements to maintain his balance. Grace pictured him plunging to the floor of the canyon, his spirit flying to meet his Maker. She couldn't breathe. Her corset was so tight! The aerialist took several steps forward, dropped to one knee, and sat on the rope.

One of Leon's assistants had raced to fix the dangling support line. Then, a cry of alarm came up from the gorge and spread like wildfire through the nervous crowd. The line had been cut!

"Who would do such a thing?" Grace gasped.

Blake looked grave. "Perhaps one of those who bet against the professor."

"*That's* why I don't like gambling!" she exclaimed, glaring up into his face. "Greed is such an ugly motivator; it could cause that man to die!" She jabbed her fan towards the figure still sitting on the wire.

Mr. Greene had the good sense to remain silent. Men filed down into the gorge to serve as lookouts for the other ropes, while the damaged one was retied. Grace imagined herself in the professor's position. Would *she* be ready to meet her Maker? A deep shiver coursed through her, and a tiny flicker of realization lit inside her head. Daniel wasn't the only one with much to settle.

Suddenly she realized how much she needed him. Intrinsically she knew he pointed to truth. He had answers. That was one reason she found him stabilizing as well as fascinating. Grace realized at that moment that she would do anything—give up her career, her dreams of singing *Aïda* to adoring fans, the promise of wealth and acclaim—to be by Daniel's side. He completed her. *He* was a sure bet.

With this, it felt as if a heavy weight lifted from her chest and drifted silently into the blue sky. She sank down onto her stool, light-headed.

"He's moving!"

Grace saw Professor Leon rising ever so slowly to his feet. As he began to inch toward them again, he looked angry, and he was talking to himself. Finally, finally, he stepped onto Lover's Leap. The whole thing had taken less than a half hour. As soon as her husband's safety was guaranteed, Mrs. St. John collapsed in a heap of bustled skirts and petticoats. Grace could barely see what was happening around all the clamoring people. Word spread that the woman was revived and Leon's personal physician and crowd members argued against the aerialist making a return trip, which he had been contracted to do. To his credit, Mr. Young agreed with them. The family was trundled off to their rooms at The Grand View, and Grace sought hers at The Cliff House.

* * *

A building sense of excitement and confidence had left Grace unable to nap. Instead, she had laid on the now-familiar bed and thought. She imagined different scenarios and how she would respond, what she would say. For the more she pondered it, the more sure she was that a man with Daniel Monroe's sense of honor would not ignore a lady's direct plea for a conference. He would know she was distressed. He was too considerate to leave her in that state indefinitely.

She must be beautiful. Grace didn't have to think long on what to wear. There was an evening dress of gold silk with "Watkins, New York" on the label that cried out for redemption. She had failed in it before: but it was a gown meant for triumphant moments. This time would be different.

When she was ready, Grace knocked softly on her aunt's door. A voice called for her to enter. Martha was reclining on her chaise lounge.

"Good, I'm glad I didn't have to press you to join the party tonight," she said. "Mr. Greene is growing impatient with your 'headaches.'"

"Yes, he asked me to meet him at eight." She didn't add that she had ordered a dinner tray to her room to avoid the possibility of having to take that meal alone with Blake.

"I hope you've tired of your games and put that preacher out of your mind. It's time to stop thinking about summer romances."

"Why would you oppose a match between myself and Rev. Monroe?" asked Grace, mentally girding herself for battle.

Her aunt chortled. "A match? Ha!"

"Why not? You saw yourself the type of family from which he comes."

Martha surveyed her with more careful consideration, as if

weighing her niece's gravity. "For a local girl, yes, I admit he could be considered a catch. I agree his family has money and charm. Even old money. But you need to think of your future, all you've worked for. Would you throw all that away to be some backwoods preacher's wife? To live on his salary? Never to publicly sing again? And maybe even to follow him to God-knows-what forsaken place to preach to the heathen?"

"Yes."

The word, calm but undoubtedly firm, fell like a pin drop in the room. Martha stared at her for a minute, then closed her eyes, raised her brows, and drew in a deep breath as though to retreat from the reality just spoken. She waved a hand in Grace's direction. "I can't deal with you just now, Grace. Not when you're making no sense like this." But the next second the act of weakness was gone. Martha's eyes popped open and her voice sharpened. "But you'd better be prepared to give Mr. Greene the answer he deserves. Don't you dare reject him foolishly after the way you've strung him along."

"I'm sorry if I've encouraged Blake to no end," Grace replied more softly. "But I never felt for him what I do for Daniel. I knew something was missing…I just didn't know what. Now I know what it feels like to love someone so much you can hardly breathe."

"Balderdash! Sentimental mumbo-jumbo! Security is what lasts! A woman must make her own accomplishments, so she is never helpless! A woman must have money, money of her own! Everything else is unreliable!"

Grace's brow puckered as she suddenly heard her aunt's vulnerability speaking. She dropped to a sitting position on the edge of the settee. "Are you saying that because you care about me— because you don't want to see what happened to my mother happen to me? Because of what happened to *you*? Daniel is not like my father, Aunt. He would never abandon the people for whom he is responsible. I think…" She paused, reflecting, then hurried on. "I think you're saying these things because being around Daniel's family made you remember all you lost. I'm sorry for all that, Aunt Martha, but I have to make my own decisions and plan for my own future. The vision of success and money in New York was never truly mine. And my heart tells me that even if I never sang another note, but I was with Daniel, I would be happy."

Martha's eyes filled with tears. Grace could hear the clock ticking on the bedside table. Then, her aunt leaned forward, and in a rare gesture of tenderness, placed her hand on Grace's shining hair. "You are so like your mother," she whispered with emphasis. "Don't make her same mistakes."

"The men with whom we fell in love are vastly different. It will be all right, Aunt Martha." Grace kissed the wrinkled fingers and rose, her skirts rustling. With a full heart, she descended to the ballroom.

Blake Greene waited for her in the lobby. His eyes lit in appreciation when he beheld her glowing appearance, and he gave her a smile that would thaw any woman's heart. She did care for him. He had infused affection into her cold world. He was fun, dashing and generous. She would have to explain things to him, but not tonight. If she could just maneuver things so that she had time alone with Daniel first...

The dancers were engaged in a lively polka-redowa as they entered. Grace managed to get a good look around the room as they went for some punch, thus ascertaining Daniel was not there yet. She suggested they take some seats near the entrance from which they could enjoy the music of the brass band and view the dancing. Blake acquiesced, but he soon grew impatient. He was the type to be on the center of the floor with a beautiful woman in his arms, not stuck on the sidelines. At last she could put him off no longer.

The music called for a hesitation waltz, a variation of the Boston. Grace and Blake had danced it together before in New York. It was just Blake's style, with its dramatic pauses, exaggerated leg movements and backbends. As they danced, Grace's train swept up on her arm, the gas lights causing her gown to shimmer like liquid gold, people gathered to watch. Only a few other couples on the periphery attempted a less vigorous form of the waltz.

"I'm glad I came," Blake told her. "I missed you."

Grace did not know how to truthfully reply. She was saved from answering when he continued.

"You're lovely. I haven't been as expressive as I should have been this past year, but I hope my presence here speaks clearly of my feelings for you."

"Yes. I—was definitely surprised. I know what it meant for you to leave your firm and travel all the way to Georgia."

"Do you?" He swept her back over his arm, one brow raised, watching her intently.

This conversation was quickly heading in the wrong direction—and in the middle of the dance floor! Had he already spoken with her father? Grace had a terrifying vision of Blake getting down on one knee and presenting her with a ring right there with everyone watching.

Her relief was too great to be expressed in mere words when she saw a black-clad figure tap Blake's shoulder. Then her eyes widened. Daniel stood there, the picture of an aristocrat, one hand behind his waist, the other tucked into a white silk embroidered vest. His dark hair was elegantly slicked back from his forehead.

Before he had a chance to speak, Blake voiced his displeasure in a single syllable: "*You?*"

Daniel bowed. "I'm sorry to interrupt, but I believe I have business with Miss Galveston."

"Couldn't it wait until after this dance?" Blake asked tersely.

"It's pressing business." A muscle in Daniel's jaw twitched. He added, "Besides, considering the ankle injury this lady recently suffered, I feared for her health."

Grace bit back a surprised laugh.

The insinuation of carelessness made Blake's face red and his posture rigid. "I would hardly have asked her to dance had I not *known* her ankle is healed…having been constantly in her company these past couple of days."

"Really, gentlemen," Grace broke in, tapping Blake with her fan to try to separate the two. She had an absurd urge to giggle. They looked like bantam roosters ready to spar. "There's really no need to make such a fuss. Mr. Greene, I'm sure it will only take a short interlude for Mr. Monroe to dispense with his 'pressing business.' Perhaps we can dance again after that."

Blake was obviously incensed at this dismissal, just when his passions had been warming toward a declaration of his intentions. But being a gentleman he could hardly argue with a lady. He backed away, expecting Grace and Daniel to also leave the dance floor.

Grace had thought the same. But as she turned in preparation to take Daniel's arm, he instead firmly drew her to him in waltz position. Their eyes met, hers round.

"The music continues," he said softly. "If you'll dance with me, I promise not to mop the floor with you like that—"

"Daniel," she cut in scoldingly.

"Just dance with me."

"I thought you didn't dance."

"Who told you that?"

As they began to waltz, Grace heard several gasps that perfectly illustrated her statement. She did giggle then. "It seems Amelia was right. She told me some of your older parishioners preferred a minister who avoided the dance floor."

"Just this one time, I'm willing to risk their censure. Who can blame a man for losing his senses over you? That's exactly what I did, not just tonight when I saw you dancing with Greene, but the first time I met you."

Grace was silent, in awe that Daniel was speaking to her in the very manner of which she had dreamed. He was holding her close, his voice soft in her ear. His steps were perfect, unfaltering, yet smaller, allowing for the weakened ankle. Thoughtful, protective, as always.

He continued. "I'm afraid I've developed a pattern of acting irrationally around you, Miss Galveston. It was completely stupid of me to storm out like I did earlier this week."

"You were taken by surprise."

"There is no excuse for my behavior. I acted—not like a gentleman, nor certainly as a Christian—but like a child."

Meeting his eyes, she shook her head. "No. You didn't. Please, it is I who have much to explain—much to tell you."

At last, the music was ending. Daniel bowed, and she curtsied.

They had ended up across the room from where Blake had retreated, and they were quite near an exit. Daniel gestured toward it. "Then I suggest we take a stroll. I need to talk with you, too, Grace."

Chapter Nine

Daniel led Grace past the porch, which was crowded with people in ball finery, onto the lawn. Water spilling from a tiered fountain splashed silver in the moonlight. Here it was quieter, and tantalizingly romantic. Daniel reminded himself he could no longer be led by his feelings. He had let things come too far, too fast. He knew all too well the biblical commandment for believers to avoid yoking with nonbelievers. But even though his determination to be honest was undergirded by two days of spiritual searching, he felt a sense of dread sitting in his stomach like a boulder.

He was debating with himself as to how he should open this conversation when Grace spoke. "I should have told you about Blake. It's true, he called on me frequently in New York. Aunt Martha is strongly in favor of a match. Until this summer, I went along with the idea, not because I really desired it, but because it seemed my most reasonable option."

"It's all right," Daniel assured her. "Like I said, I overreacted. It would be stupid of me to think you didn't have many admirers back home. Besides, it's not like any declarations have been made between us."

She stopped walking. Quickly she searched his eyes. "But— much has passed between us—nonetheless."

"It has," he agreed gravely. "And at my initiation. I'm usually much more…cautious. But what I said inside was true. For the first time where a woman was concerned, I've found myself acting first and thinking later. These past two days I've realized that—there is much we don't know about one another."

Grace nodded, touching the tip of her fan to her chin, but she looked confused. "I realize we have led very different lives," she said.

He sat down on a wrought iron bench and patted the seat beside him. Grace obliged. Thus shielded from public view by the waxy leaves of a huge magnolia tree, Daniel turned to her. "Yes, we have. And I wonder if you realize just how simple mine is, centered on home, family, and most importantly, my faith in Christ."

"Well, of course. You're a minister. Those things *must* be important to you."

"But you see, that's just it. It's not like I were a lawyer whose clients were important or a teacher whose students were important just because it's all wrapped up in my occupation, my livelihood. Not that those people may not care about their clients and students, but— what I'm trying to say is, my faith is not important to me because I'm a minister. My ministry is important to me because my faith is the core of who I am. It effects *everything* about my life. Sharing the love of God and His power of salvation with people is the central purpose of each day."

Grace smiled slightly. "Well, I don't suppose it matters which comes first, the chicken or the egg. What matters is the result—that you are who you are, and that's what I appreciate about you."

Where is this conversation going? Daniel groaned inwardly. *Lord, help me. Let me get on Your path and not get off.* He took her hand in his, looked directly into her brown eyes. He felt impatient that the soft kid of her long gloves kept him from touching her skin, and sensed in a vague, passing way that it was symbolic of a much deeper barrier that seemed to be rising between them. *Cut to the chase.* "Anyone who shares my life must have the same focus."

She swallowed, responding to the seriousness of his implication.

"Today, I realized something," she whispered. Grace proceeded slowly. "Money, acclaim, comforts—they are all empty when you possess them but are alone. I would give them all up in a second if it meant…" She stopped, drew a breath, and started again. "You talk of your life being simple. Maybe the simple things are best. I don't mind your focus on your ministry. It's admirable. I think…you probably have enough love for everyone, and enough faith for both of us." She forced a light laugh.

But Daniel was silent. He stared at his hands holding hers. *Oh, God, I did run ahead of You,* he thought. *But why, oh, why, did I—do I—feel these things for her, if it's not meant to be?*

"Please, say something."

"Whatever I say is going to be inadequate." Seconds ticked by. Her expression began to change from expectation to uncertainty. This beautiful woman had just laid her heart on the line. He was a mess inside, joy and sorrow battling because of her admission. His natural response, what he *wanted* to do, would be to take her in his arms and whisper words of love and commitment. But the part of him that was attuned to spiritual prompting urged caution. Stalling for time, he murmured, "I'm…deeply humbled that you feel that way."

Grace's brows drew together, and a trace of vulnerability trembled in her tone. "I don't want you to be humbled. I want you to be happy!"

"I am—I certainly never thought to be hearing such words from you—and I know what they cost you. I know what it would mean, what you'd be giving up, to open your heart to me. But I'm also afraid."

"Afraid? Of what?"

"That if we don't share the same priorities, our feelings may not be enough." He studied her, waiting.

"But I just told you—" Grace withdrew her hands, her back stiffening.

"Yes, about the money and the fame. I've always known you weren't that sort of person."

"Then what? I go to church every Sunday, I try to obey the

commandments and live an upstanding life. It's hardly like I'm some heathen."

"I know that. Grace, it was your gentleness, your openness—your inward as well as outward beauty that drew me. But there is more to it than that. In Ephesians it makes it clear: 'by grace are ye saved through faith; and that not of yourselves: it is the gift of God: not of works...' Even if we do good relying on our own power, we fail. It's impossible for our motivations to always be pure. It's impossible for us to do enough to save ourselves. The Bible tells us there is no one righteous. If we think we don't need God, we sin by that very attitude."

"Are you saying I'm a sinner?"

"No worse a sinner than every person, myself included. Even having submitted my life and will to God—because I know that He alone knows what is truly best for me—I fail daily. But I know the grace He extended to save me when He died for all of us on the cross covers all my sins and weaknesses, when I ask for His forgiveness and help."

"But I believe in all that—the cross, forgiveness."

"I'm sure it is true that you've heard it, but have you truly given your life to Christ?" There it was. The pivotal question.

Grace's pause lasted much too long. Finally she whispered, "I can." She looked hopeful, uncertain.

Daniel's breath came out in a ragged sigh. This he had not anticipated. What could he do with such sweetly disarming honesty? He dropped his head and jammed his fingers into his dark hair. As much as he had wanted her willingness, already having guessed the answer would not be a straight "yes," his emotions were much too tied up in this.

"What?" she urged softly.

"Just as it's impossible for *me* to have enough faith to save *you*, this can't be something you do because of somebody else. It has to be because you truly want Christ in your life. And I wonder...you've been so hurt by your father...there's so much more you need to know about God."

"I can learn. Isn't it enough that I'm willing?"

102

"Yes, it's enough, but are you ready? Perhaps we should just take some time here. There's a lot to talk about, and maybe Amelia would be a good person to—"

But Grace had stood up. Her face was pale, and she trembled visibly. Her breath came in tiny gasps. Daniel watched her, feeling like a man facing down a locomotive, knowing he didn't want to hear what she was about to say yet unable to stop it.

"I tell you everything about my past, even the most humiliating details. I open up my heart and hold nothing back. I confess to you that I am willing to give up everything in my current life so that I can be by your side. You tell me I'm a sinner, and even then I am willing to pray this magic prayer that will make me acceptable to you. You lead me along...and then you slam the door in my face!"

Daniel stood. "Grace, please listen. I only thought—"

But she would hear no more from him. She held up her hand, her eyes blazing. "No, you didn't think! And neither did I. I never dreamed the good, kind Rev. Monroe could be so judgmental, so cruel. Yes, my father has hurt me, but never so much as you. *He* never pretended to feel or be anything besides what he was."

Daniel felt like the torrent of her words had created a chasm in his heart as deep as the gorge a few hundred feet away. "The last thing I wanted to do was hurt you," he said.

"Ah, famous last words. Couldn't you think of something more original than that?" Grace laughed bitterly. She was so cold, so untouchable now. "Well, I suppose I deserve them. Maybe I've been the more foolish of the two of us because all this time, despite all we have said—you never once even told me you loved me."

"I love you."

His words were softly spoken, his arms hanging limp and helpless at his sides. He wanted to embrace her but couldn't. This encounter had underlined the truth, not changed it. For a moment, though, as she stirred slightly, he knew she sensed the magic and the truth of what he said, and he dared to hope. Once more he suggested, "Maybe if we just took some time, looked into the Bible about some of these things..."

Grace's expression instantly congealed, and she took a step back. "At least in New York," she replied, "they thought I was good enough." Then she turned and fled into the hotel.

* * *

An oil lamp burned all night in a small Victorian cottage on the outskirts of Tallulah Falls. The house was new and fairly attractive, even boasting some of that gingerbread trim that was all the rage. A generous parishioner let it to Rev. Daniel Monroe for practically a pittance. Not that Daniel's father couldn't have bought the place several times over, but Daniel liked to make his own way. It earned the respect of the townsfolk and gave him a sense of autonomy.

A man—even a bachelor—did have a mother, though. Inside, while the house was still rather sparsely furnished, the touches of Evelyn Monroe were readily apparent. She had insisted on her younger son having certain pieces of furniture, and she had graced the bare walls with a few choice paintings. Daniel had to admit that did make the quiet little place feel a bit more like home. He had even dreamed of one day bringing a wife here. Now, that possibility felt more remote than ever.

The first woman for whom he had ever entertained more than a passing interest believed he disdained her. She thought he had led her on only to crush her with holier-than-thou, cold-hearted rejection. Maybe he had led her on. But if so it had only been because he was a man, a human, who had been following his own heart. Daniel would be the first to admit that the sickening scene in the garden was greatly his own fault.

Still, how could Grace have misjudged him so? He hated to be misunderstood, but even more than that, he hated the hurt in her eyes. He hated that the way it looked right now, he could possibly lose her forever.

Why had this happened? Why had he even met Grace if this was to be the end result? It felt like God had dangled a carrot in front of his face only to jerk it away. He pushed that idea aside. He knew God better than that. His Father, as he had told Grace, was loving and kind, working even what seemed like disasters out for good and for His glory. Daniel was hardly a new convert, and as young as he was, he was still not a completely untested believer. His faith wouldn't founder at the first sign of a disappointment. Still, it seemed almost impossible to reckon with the possibility that God's ultimate plan might include something like Daniel's words planting seeds in Grace's heart, rather than a continuing relationship. Why couldn't somebody else plant those seeds? Why couldn't he have come along after the harvest, able to reap a beautiful bride?

All night he struggled with such questions, searching the Word of God, praying. What could he say to Grace? At last, as he realized that, as usual, the wisest choice was to leave it in God's hands, he felt a still, small voice say to his heart: *Pray for her.*

All right, Lord, he surrendered. *But in the morning, would it hurt to talk to Amelia? She's probably the only one Grace will listen to now.*

Before Daniel could determine an answer, he fell asleep. Dawn was just streaking the horizon with faint color.

* * *

The churning of his empty stomach awoke him. Daniel sat up. He had been sprawled on the chair next to his kitchen table, draped over the open Bible. His back and neck were killing him. He blew out the lamp and looked at the clock. Right at noon.

He didn't really want to face people, but there was little in his house to eat. Besides, the thought of cooking in his present emotional state was just too much. He wondered how his stomach could go on like everything was normal when his heart felt like it had been crushed into a wad of waste paper. He'd have to go to the café. Maybe he'd get lucky and find a table in the corner. But first he'd have to change. He was still wearing his white dress shirt and the fine black worsted wool trousers that matched his tailcoat.

Emerging a few minutes later in gray pants and vest and with his hair combed, Daniel squinted at the bright light. The bad thing about being the local minister was that he wasn't allowed to ever have a bad day. Everyone recognized him, waved to him, and expected his cheerful response and sincere inquiries into their health, both spiritual and physical.

He had to pass Wylie's Refreshments en route. He glimpsed Amelia inside in a sensible brown dress, handing a customer an ice cream sundae with a cherry on top. He thought about stopping to talk to her. *After lunch*, he decided.

But just as he passed the building, Daniel heard her voice, calling his name. He stopped and turned, noting her worried frown as she approached.

"You look awful," she announced with her usual tact.

"Thanks."

"Listen, I think you should know, I've…seen Grace."

"You have?" Daniel was instantly alert.

Amelia wiped her hands on her ruffled apron. Or was it more wringing than wiping? "Yes. This morning. She told me a little about what had happened last night. I tried to explain things, help her see it from your viewpoint, but…"

"She was still too angry to listen?"

Amelia nodded, her mouth drawn into a flat line of sympathy and regret.

Daniel took his hat off, rubbed his hand over his face, then replaced the bowler. "Well, maybe in a few days," he suggested lamely.

Now Amelia's head shook. "Daniel, I don't think so. Grace sent a message for me to come early this morning, and not just because she wanted to talk. She said goodbye. She left on the ten o'clock train."

"*What?*"

"I'm sorry. I did all I could to dissuade her, but her mind was made up. I think her aunt and Mr. Greene were all too happy to oblige, even though it was inconvenient to leave so quickly. They didn't ask any questions. Anything to get her away from you. Mr. Greene even paid some outlandish price to buy tickets off a family. You know how many people are leaving town today."

Daniel took hold of Amelia's arms to stop her. "Why didn't you come get me?" he demanded.

He was a bit too rough, for Amelia drew back in offense. "And how would that look?" she questioned.

"Sorry," he muttered. His gaze fell on the tracks that gleamed in the distance, leading south. His mind was still churning. "Where did she go? Home?"

"Mr. Greene was eager to offer a few weeks in Newport at his uncle's estate. Grace spoke of Monsieur LeMonte joining them there, resuming her daily practice. Getting ready for fall season."

"Mr. Greene, Mr. Greene!" Daniel burst out, his fists balled up. *He'll have her*, he thought in despair. He kept looking at the tracks, as if he might grab a horse and ride after the train. No, that was stupid. Even if he caught up with her in Athens or Atlanta, there was nothing new he could say. Only God could make a difference now. If their love was meant to be, He could redeem Grace and bring her back. His shoulders slumped, and his breath exhaled in a deep sigh.

Amelia's eyes were filled with pity. She placed a gentle hand on his arm. "I'm sorry, Daniel," she said again.

"It's all right, Amelia."

"What are you going to do now?"

That answer was, at last, easy. "Pray for her."

Chapter Ten

November 18, 1886

My Dearest Amelia,
Well, I did it! I sang Aïda *to a sold-out house six days ago. And in German, no less. Monsieur LeMonte's coaching and string-pulling paid off. It was indeed a glorious moment. Since then I've been deluged with roses and chocolates, and the calling cards and invitations pile up in our tray. I can hardly appear in public without being accosted. But for all the flattery and sense of accomplishment, something is missing. It's your sweet, genuine face. Out of the many people I have met this year, you are the only one I would consider a friend.*

I was surprised but happy to hear that Richard Callaway has been writing to you. I knew he really took a liking to you at Aunt Fannie's; I just never would have guessed he had the gumption to follow through. I know he's kind and you share some interests, but do you think he's exciting enough for you, Amelia, dear? Maybe if he visits again next summer as he hopes to do, you'll be able to tell.

Your letters have meant the world to me these past months, but I'm afraid they will no longer suffice. I'm enclosing train tickets for you and your parents and begging you, come spend Thanksgiving with us. We'll arrange a special box at the opera. We'll go to Tiffany's, Central Park and The Statue of Liberty. You deserve to experience all the pleasures and sights of New York City. Please don't say no. Wire me when you are coming.

Your friend,
Grace Galveston

Grace folded the gold-embossed page of stationery and dropped it, along with three tickets, into the envelope. She licked it and rang for the maid.

Ever since their return to New York, her time had been full. When she had not been engaged in practice, Blake had escorted her to parties and dinners and taken her for drives to view the brilliant autumn foliage of the surrounding countryside. She and Aunt Martha had shopped for the newest cool weather fashions. Once Grace's father had learned of her acceptance in the role of Aïda, his attentions had renewed. He had belittled his disinterest in her summer escape by declaring he had known the North Georgia air would be her perfect cure. Grace knew the air had worked no wonders. Before, her vulnerability had left her open to attacks of nerves, leaving her powerless to sing. Now, she had closed up like a creature in a shell, protected by her anger. She was well along the road to eventual bitterness. But this she didn't realize. She only knew the anger drove her along. And, completely ignorant of his daughter's inner workings, Hampton had hastily attempted to bridge the gap between them with regular invitations to his Fifth Avenue home, an order for two Worth gowns and a stunning set of emerald jewelry. He would hear no protests. He wanted to make sure that his own involvement in Grace's success should not go unaccredited. At least that was Grace's suspicion. She could not allow his shallow overtures to arouse hope. Her heart had opened and been crushed too many times, most recently in a devastating fashion. It was Daniel's fault. She refused to think back to the sharpness of her heartache when she had first left Tallulah Falls, the empty days without sight of his face and the long nights when she would lie awake and painstakingly go over in her mind every word, every look they had shared, trying to find somewhere to lay the blame for his rejection. Yet, even now, as much as Grace attempted to fill her time to crowd out thoughts of him, she could not ignore the empty spot that still ached inside her.

Amelia was the answer. She was stable, caring and fun. A perfect distraction. Grace could not wait to throw open her door to find her friend standing there.

When Maureen appeared in her gray frock, Grace handed her the envelope and said, "Please post this at once."

* * *

Amelia came. During the off-season it had not proven difficult for her father to close up shop. Grace basked in showing her friend all her favorite places and watching her awed responses. The crowds were larger, the buildings taller, and the amusements were more sophisticated than the Wylies had ever experienced. They were especially enthralled with the spectacle of the opera—the lavish scenes and costumes, the glinting jewels, the heart-stopping, soaring voices. They had Thanksgiving dinner with the Galvestons. Such an elegant repast had never been seen even in Tallulah's fine hotels.

But as much as Amelia openly enjoyed this vacation of a lifetime, even letting Grace dress her up like a high-society debutante, she was not swept away. She kept her head. She was the same down-to-earth, unselfish girl from the mountains. And Grace loved her for it.

The last evening of Amelia's visit was to leave the greatest impression on Grace. During the short time they had together, Grace had adroitly maneuvered conversations and circumstances so that she and Amelia had no chance to stagnate on the topic of Daniel. Now, though, knowing her friend was leaving the following day, Grace felt a tugging at her heart. Her guard was down.

As they nibbled cookies and drank milk in Grace's bedroom, Maureen delivered a gift-wrapped box. The message accompanying it had read simply, "A small adornment for my most precious jewel."

Maureen, who stood over her mistress, gasped when Grace

sprung the latch. A diamond necklace glinted in the light. Amelia rose to see what the fuss was about.

"Who is it from?" she asked.

"Blake, of course." Grace held the beautiful gems up to her slender throat, admiring the effect. Then she shook her head, replaced the necklace, and snapped the lid shut. She held it out to Maureen. "Send it back."

"Ma'am?"

"He knows full well I can't accept such a gift without committing to marry him first. He's merely reminding me of the riches with which he'll shower me when I agree to become his bride."

Maureen retreated obediently, taking the box with her. But Amelia, who appeared bewildered by Grace's matter-of-fact tone, drew near. "*When*?" she repeated.

Grace turned on her dressing table stool, feeling almost apologetic, though for the life of her she didn't know why. "I told you in a letter how he proposed at Newport. Don't you remember? I made him promise to give me until Christmas for an answer."

"I thought then that pressing his advantage when you were hurt by another was—not right. I think now that plying you with expensive gifts is nothing short of bribery." Amelia put her hands on her hips. Clad in a cutwork lace nightgown and wrapper, she looked like an avenging angel.

Grace looked at her for a minute, never having thought of it quite that way, then laughed. "Oh, Amelia. How I'm going to miss your plain speaking." She shrugged. "But why shouldn't I marry him? Despite what you may think, he *has* changed. He's become much more thoughtful and caring—and patient, agreeing to wait all this time."

"At least he's smart enough to act that way until he has you."

"Well, who would you have me marry?"

"No one, unless you love them."

Grace's gaze fell to the Persian carpet. Softly she said, "The one I loved wouldn't have me."

Amelia bit her lip. Grace was glad she was quiet; she didn't want a repeat of how difficult the parting had been for Daniel, a listing of all the reasons he had not felt free to propose to her. In her opinion that was all a bunch of super-spiritual nonsense. She had registered her protest by refusing to attend church since returning to New York. But God didn't seem moved by her strike.

"Anyway," she went on, "even if he came to me tomorrow on bent knee, I wouldn't have him. I wouldn't be able to trust him now any more than I do my father. No, I'm planning to accept Blake's proposal when he repeats it at Christmas. I care deeply for him, and the match makes perfect sense. Aunt Martha was right all along."

When she looked up, she was shocked to see tears filling Amelia's eyes—and running over! She was further taken aback when the girl knelt in front of her and took her hands.

"Grace," she said, "*I'm* here on bent knee, and I hope you'll listen to me."

Grace tried to shake her off, but Amelia was not to be put off. "No," she continued. "I've tried to say this before, but it seemed you didn't want to hear it. You've been so kind to me during my visit, but somehow you haven't been the same. Well, I'm going home tomorrow, so listen anyway. My heart breaks over how hurt you've been, and how little love you've received. No wonder you're afraid of it! Your father has been wrong, crazy—and blind. Daniel—maybe he made mistakes, too, but he's just a man, a man who's in love with you and doesn't know what to do about it. Everyone messes up. Everyone will at some time disappoint you. As much as I want to always be your friend, some day I might, too. There's only one Person who will *never* let you down."

Knowing what Amelia meant, Grace said, "God is not a person."

"Of course He is—in the God-man Jesus Christ, who promises that He will be a friend who sticks closer than a brother. Wait here."

Amelia got up suddenly, wiping her eyes, and scurried off toward her own bedroom. Grace was too stunned to disobey her. Moments later Amelia returned, clutching a worn brown book. She laid it reverently in Grace's lap. Grace turned questioning eyes upon her.

"My Bible. Actually my first Bible. I used it a lot when I was a young teenager." Seeing Grace was about to protest, she held up a hand. "Don't worry, I have a new one now. This one will be of better use here with you. You'll notice I underlined a lot of passages and wrote in the margins. The Books of John and Romans are especially good."

She paused as if waiting for Grace to start thumbing through the pages on the spot. Grace didn't want to take the book, much less look through it, but she didn't want to hurt Amelia's feelings, either. She looked so hopeful and vulnerable standing there wringing her hands.

"It will give you answers, Grace, it really will. It will show you God loves you and longs to heal your hurts and fill the hole in your heart."

How had Amelia known? Grace went to great lengths to keep anyone from suspecting that she felt so empty on the inside.

"Say something," Amelia urged.

"Thank you."

"You will keep it, and look at it?"

Grace nodded.

"And write me any questions you might have?"

"I will."

Amelia smiled. She looked relieved. "Thank *you*, Grace, for making my dream of coming to New York come true. I've had such a wonderful time. You've been—you *are*—like a sister to me. Even though we may be miles apart, you'll always be a dear friend." Impulsively she bent down and threw her arms around Grace's mute form.

Grace was so overcome by surprise at Amelia's open-hearted speech and gesture that she sat on her dressing table stool, holding the Bible, long after her guest had gone off to bed.

* * *

Over a week later, Grace stood at her bedroom window looking out over Gramercy Park. It was a cold, gray day, but even the icy gusts of wind did not discourage the many citizens out on their holiday errands. She watched the passing carriages of shoppers and merry-makers with an expression far from cheer.

It had been a troubling day. Earlier, Aunt Martha had insisted on the two of them going to view a flat on Fifth Avenue owned by a friend of Hampton's who had indicated he would make them a nice arrangement. Martha had been ecstatic, all but promising the friend's agent that they were interested. She had practically refused to listen to Grace's reservations.

If I protest outright, she'll have to comply, thought Grace. After all, it was her money and her father's money involved. But Grace did not like to dictate to her older relative. It seemed disrespectful of Martha's position and the years of her life she had given as Grace's guardian. Martha would at least have to listen to her concerns, though…maybe later tonight when she returned from her round of visits.

Grace's mind ran through the 1850s row house that had been her only home—the long front parlor with the dining room behind on the main floor, the dumb waiter near the stairs to the basement, and the informal dining room, kitchen and laundry below. Behind there was a quaint garden. The house possessed white marble mantels and lovely plasterwork on the ceilings. And while the walnut and mahogany of the floors and built-in appointments might not be as fashionable now as the lighter woods were, Grace found them warm and comforting.

The fact that the brownstone fronted on the private park made it an appealing lot amongst its 66 Gramercy neighbors. A man named Ruggles had bought the land in the 1830s. In order to develop it, he'd had to drain the marshy site first, but his efforts had paid off. The neighborhood had been quickly occupied by important professionals and politicians. It had not been a home Hampton need be embarrassed to bring his bride to. Knowing that Louisa had lived here—if only for a few short months—was at the heart of Grace's desire to remain. It was the only link she had with her mother. In these rooms Louisa had walked and slept and for a few short hours before her death, had held her newborn daughter. Here, too, Maum Sally had trained Grace in manners and morals, her presence, her stories, a constant reminder of Louisa. This place was all that was familiar. There had been some changes around them, true. Some of the first apartment buildings in the city had been raised in these environs, notably those at 129 East 17th Street and the Gramercy at 34 Gramercy Park East. And the area was now home to many performing and visual artists. Grace thought that she still fit in here just fine.

A knock sounded on her door, which was open. She turned to see Maureen standing there. "Your father is here to see you, Miss," she said.

Her father...another obstacle to remaining in this house.

"Please prepare a tea tray, Maureen."

Minutes later Grace descended to the parlor. Her father had his back turned. Between his fingers he held the card that had been attached to a bouquet of yellow roses. He gave the flowers an idle sniff. Grace cleared her throat, and he turned. *Still so handsome at almost 50...no wonder my mother agreed to go north with him,* Grace thought. Hampton's dark hair was streaked with silver. His angular features were set off by an elegant black morning coat and tailored gray trousers, a fit physique, and a commanding manner. At the sight of his daughter, he broke into a grin.

"It looks like a wake in here," he commented, gesturing to the veritable bower of arrangements sent by Grace's admirers.

Grace laughed and spread her hands helplessly. "They just keep coming," she said.

Hampton stuck the card back amongst the roses. "I'm afraid the scent is rather overpowering."

"That's why they're all here and not in my room."

"Speaking of rooms, how did you like the flat?" His eyes lit with anticipation as he drew closer to her.

"Er—it was lovely. Quite fashionable."

Hampton grinned again. "No sense making the delivery men drive all the way to Gramercy Park, eh? Besides, you'll be much more in your element on Fifth."

"Will I? You didn't seem to think so until this fall."

As soon as the words were out, Grace bit her lip. This was not the approach she had meant to take. She had been reading the Bible Amelia had left with her and had been greatly impressed by the gentle Savior portrayed in John—and the way He used love to reach people. In Romans, she had found exhortations to "bless those who persecute you" and not to be overcome by evil "but overcome evil with good." Her study had also brought back to her mind much that Maum Sally had taught her, including many Proverbs like "A soft answer turns away wrath, but a harsh word stirs up anger."

The darkening clouds of her father's expression were held at bay by the arrival of the tea tray. With shaking hands she poured the hot liquid into two china teacups.

"Look," her father said, as if noticing her discomfiture, "I'm trying to make up for the wrongs of the past by doing right by you now."

"Then let me stay here."

"Here? Why?"

"*Why*? This is *home*!" Grace gestured around the room with her spoon. Frustrated, she plunked in a lump of sugar and stirred. "I like it here. I like the neighbors, I like the quiet, and most of all I like the fact that I've lived here all my life."

"Don't you think it's time to move beyond your childhood?"

Grace stared mutely at this man tied to her so closely by blood but really little more than a stranger—silently imploring him to realize how the lack of support during that very era had created such vulnerability now. When he merely stared back, she voiced another question. "And what if I fail? What if I don't continue on this path to stardom? How much will I belong on Fifth Avenue then?"

"You won't fail."

"But if I do—or if I'm unable to sing? Will you want to pay for that flat then?"

Hampton looked uncomfortable. He shifted in his seat, his tea untouched. "What you suggest is ridiculous, but if some emergency, some bad thing, were to happen, of course I would see you located wherever your needs were best served."

The master of the vague answer, thought Grace. Bitterness made her add aloud, "Of course you wouldn't want me near you then."

"Look, what do you want from me, Grace? To move into my house? That would hardly be appropriate, with your maiden aunt in tow."

"No! I want to stay here!"

"Fine! No one's pushing you out, though I must admit I've never seen anyone more resistive to advancement."

"Perhaps our priorities just aren't the same," Grace replied, then started inwardly as she realized Daniel had used almost those same words with her.

Disgruntled, Hampton sat back in his wing chair and sipped the hot tea. "Just don't throw out the idea, Grace. Take some more time and think it over. Consider the fact that the right address would not hurt your prospects any."

"Remember, I'm supposed to give Blake an answer this month. I hardly see why there's such a clamor to move considering that."

Hampton eyed her shrewdly. "So you've decided to accept him?"

"I thought I had," Grace said softly, her mind drifting.

"*Thought?*"

"I have been planning to accept, but—oh, I don't want to talk about it…"

"Well, even if you do say yes, you'll have a long period of engagement with all the social activities that entails. Once people know you're to definitely become a Greene you'll be even more sought-after socially. During that time, it will make sense for you to live close to me and your new circle of friends."

"With all that change before me, it seems all the more reason to stay securely in my own nest for a while."

"By the saints, you're a stubborn girl," Hampton exclaimed suddenly, laughing.

She laughed, too. "Wonder where I got that from?"

To her surprise, Hampton answered without hesitation, "Your mother."

"You almost never talk about her. I've learned almost everything

I know from Maum Sally and Aunt Martha. Why?"

"Some things are best left in the past."

"But don't you see, I need to know."

"*What* do you need to know?"

Grace was nervous, wanting to take advantage of this rare moment and this tenuous link between them, but afraid if she pressed too far, he would withdraw. She ventured, "Everything... anything...but most especially, did you love her?"

If Grace had expected him to instantly declare it had been so, she was disappointed. But a spark came into his eyes, and she saw it before he could retreat behind his mask of indifference. It made her imagine him younger, more rash, more vital. The way he had looked to her mother. The way he had been before abdicating his role in *her* life. He stared into space, into the past, as he spoke. "We had a rocky relationship, your mother and I. I saved her from a miserable fate but brought her into even more trouble. She never let me forget I was the enemy. Was it love or hate? I think, for me, if love is not being able to imagine life without that person...if losing them means trying every day to forget them...then I loved her."

Grace was silent a long time, digesting these words she had waited for so long to hear. They sank like water into her parched soul. But she was not satisfied. There was one more question that had surged with her every heartbeat for as long as she could remember.

"And...did you love me?" she whispered.

"I never blamed you for her loss. If I blamed anyone, it was myself."

"But then...why...?" Grace could not bring herself to finish the question. *Why did you move back home and leave us? Why didn't you take me with you? Why the infrequent visits, the distant manners, the lonely birthdays and Christmases? Why was I treated like your stepchild?* She felt like her heart would break with the longing. She didn't have to say all those things. He knew.

Hampton turned anguished eyes upon her. "Have you ever seen a picture of your mother?"

Grace shook her head. Any likenesses of Louisa had been destroyed in the fire.

"Every day you grew more like her. Now you have but to look in the mirror."

As if he could stand no more, he leaped to his feet and strode to the door. His face was set as he gathered up his great coat, hat, scarf and walking stick. But there was a strange new urging in her spirit, so that Grace knew she could not let him leave without saying one thing more. With tears in her eyes, she followed him to the foyer and stood in the parlor doorway.

"Father, I forgive you."

"What?" He turned to stare at her in amazement.

"I've been reading the Bible, and a dear friend told me that I had to let go of all the hurt inside. I can't keep being afraid of disappointing you. I can't keep being angry. I want to be free. I don't want to be bitter. So—" she took a deep, gulping breath—"for everything—I forgive you."

With those words, Grace felt like she had the day Leon had crossed the gorge, as if a great weight had lifted off her chest and drifted up into the sky. She knew it was the power in the words of Amelia's Bible that had encouraged her, enabled her, to do this. She might have hoped for tears or a hug, if not a belated apology. But Hampton wasn't ready for that. He looked...terrified. With no more spoken he jammed his hat on his head and left the house. So it had to be enough for now, this feeling of release.

Weakly, Grace dragged herself up to her bedroom and closed the door. There on a little table lay the open Bible. Next to it was her rocking chair, and it was there she promptly collapsed, with her head cradled on its seat, and wept.

A long time later she reached for the book. Wiping her eyes on her shawl, she thumbed again through the pages of Romans, where certain passages stood out, underlined a long time ago by her dear friend: "for all have sinned, and come short of the glory of God," "but God commendeth His love toward us, in that, while we were yet sinners, Christ died for us," and "for the wages of sin is death; but the gift of God is eternal life through Jesus Christ our Lord." And finally: "if thou shalt confess with thy mouth the Lord Jesus, and shalt believe in thine heart that God hath raised him from the dead, thou shalt be saved."

"I surrender, Lord," Grace said out loud. "I give it all up, my hurts, my dreams, my fears. I don't want to live life like this anymore. Nothing else—no one else—has filled this terrible empty place inside my heart. Can You? If You can, I'll do whatever You want with the rest of my life."

Instantly she sank to the floor, spent, then surrounded and filled with the most indescribable sense of peace and perfect love.

Chapter Eleven

Daniel learned of the death of Saul Jones on a Saturday. On Sunday morning he had to deliver a message he had already prepared that had been intended to warm hearts for the coming celebration of Christ's birth. It was not an easy thing, for Mr. Jones had been a favorite parishioner. He had supported the fledgling minister from the time Daniel's name was considered for Trinity Church. And even when crippled by advanced rheumatism, he had attended faithfully, always ready with a word of encouragement and a twinkle in his eye.

By Sunday afternoon the body had been laid in the receiving parlor, and the family had gathered. They were prepared for the traditional rites of mourning with a black ribbon on the doorknob, the mirrors covered with black crepe, and a vigil candle burning next to the coffin. Mrs. Jones met Daniel at the door, arrayed in black; she would continue to dress in the various stages of mourning—finally graduating to gray and lavender—for about two-and-a-half years.

Daniel had been a frequent visitor in the Jones home, often having Sunday lunch and staying to play checkers or chess with Saul. So it didn't surprise him when Elizabeth Jones hugged his neck and burst into tears, despite the popular notion that a new widow should stoically "hold up." He patted her back, a lump rising in his throat at the sight of the dear woman's grief.

At last she pulled back and wiped her wrinkled cheeks with a damp handkerchief. "Ah, Rev. Monroe," she sighed, "'tis a hard thing."

"I know it is, Mrs. Jones."

"Even though we'd known for some time his heart was weak—well, a woman's never prepared for her husband to die."

"He died in his sleep?"

She nodded. "And looks more peaceable now than I've seen him in years, what with the rheumatism."

Daniel went with her into the receiving parlor, where he sat for some time with the family, praying with them and comforting them with some words of Scripture. There were quiet tears but no agonized sobbing. Mrs. Jones summed up the reason for that when at last Daniel rose to leave.

"We thank you for coming by, Rev. Monroe. It's always a help to us how you care. We know all you say is true—that Saul is with the Lord now. And that's the biggest comfort of all."

Donning his hat and overcoat, Daniel left the house. Snowflakes had begun to fall. It was early for snow. It made for a beautiful scene as he walked back toward town.

He pulled his lapels up around his neck, thinking of the Jones family. The biggest challenge ahead of Elizabeth was not settling any question of Saul's eternal destiny, but of releasing her best friend to the Lord and finding the strength to face each day without him. They had enjoyed a long and fruitful life together. That's what Daniel had always hoped for, a soul mate, a partner.

It was not going to be easy, officiating over Saul's funeral on the morrow, then going ahead with a string of advent sermons and celebrations. He was definitely lacking any vestige of holiday cheer. For Christmas his brother and sister-in-law would visit from Darien. That would make three happy couples at Crown Pointe, plus Daniel. He simply didn't want to face any of it.

The Lord seemed to whisper in his ear: *When you are weak, I am strong.*

I know, God, he argued back. Hadn't he practically lived all autumn on the promise in Jeremiah that God wanted not to harm him, but to give him a future and a hope? *I know You are enough. But I can't help it, I want human companionship, too. Is it so wrong to wish for a helpmate?* He was so lonely, his steps almost turned toward the town. He knew there would be a cozy little gathering around the wood stove at Wylie's. They would be talking and laughing and drinking hot chocolate. The one person who understood how he felt would be there. His mother had gently urged him to start looking for romance closer to home. While she had liked Grace and had quickly discerned the spark between Grace and her son, she simply couldn't bear to witness Daniel's continuing sadness. If he went to Wylie's now, he reasoned, and asked Amelia to take a walk with him in the snow, she would know. She would realize that he was attempting to move towards something more than friendship. Maybe the passion he didn't feel now would come with time.

But instead Daniel found himself cutting off the main road on the path that led to Lover's Leap. As he trudged through the woods, the dead leaves under his feet receiving their slow baptism of silent white flakes, he thought about the talk he'd had with Amelia after she'd returned from New York. He had been so encouraged to learn that Grace had accepted the Bible from their mutual friend. He knew God could work wonders once His Word got into a person's hands. But then Amelia had gone on, with her gentle honesty, to describe Grace's glittering lifestyle, Blake's ardent courtship, and the statement made by Grace herself of her intentions to marry the young lawyer.

"Keep praying," Amelia had told him, "but I just don't want to raise any false hopes. Even if she finds the Lord, it may be that she never leaves New York."

And the part that she left unsaid: *It may be that she marries Blake.* For even though Daniel was willing to move north, that would not matter if Blake had already managed to capture her heart. After all, Blake had been there all this time to generously spread his sympathy and attention like salve on her wounds.

When he reached the overlook, Daniel sat down on a fallen log and removed a photograph from his vest pocket. Grace, clinging to his arm as they stood on this very spot, smiled at him in sepia tones. He was glad she had been laughing when Hunnicutt took the picture, instead of striking a traditionally somber pose. It made her so much more life-like. He could almost see the roses in her cheeks and smell the sweet fragrance of her hair as he had on that special day.

For the hundredth time Daniel asked God to remove his longing for this woman if their love was not meant to be.

He heard a rustle behind him but dismissed it as a squirrel. Daniel continued with his prayers. But the next moment, when a voice spoke, he was startled into jumping up and turning quickly.

"The locals say that at this very spot, an Indian maiden leaped off the precipice after the man she loved, unwilling to live without him."

The picture that met his eyes was so amazing Daniel thought he must be hallucinating. Before him stood the very object of his thoughts. Grace's red-gold hair and brown eyes were exquisitely framed in a hooded cloak of white fur that fell blow her knees and made her seem a product of the snowy surroundings. A figment of his imagination. He jammed the photo back into his vest and stood staring at her, mouth slightly open.

"I guess I understand how she felt," Grace added softly.

"What—how are you here?" he asked dumbly.

"Train," she said, raising one brow in a teasing gesture. "I wired Amelia that I was coming. She told me where you were when I got here, so I walked out to meet you. I saw you turn off the road."

His heart started to beat again. He took a step forward. Suddenly, the meaning of her words about the Indian maiden dawned on him, and the blood went rushing through his veins. He managed to keep his voice calm. "I guess what I meant to ask was *why* did you come? It's hardly tourist season."

She smiled, and he was struck by the tranquility radiating from her. "I had to tell you in person that I made peace with my Father."

"You did? Why, that's wonderful, Grace! Did he come with you?"

Again, the enigmatic smile that left him bemused. "I guess you could say so." Then she laughed, and put a gloved hand to her heart. In the face of Daniel's obvious confusion, she clarified, "I didn't mean that father...although I did forgive him for everything in the past. I meant *our* Father."

"Oh, Grace! Thank God!" Joy overpowered Daniel's confusion, and he leaped forward, grabbing her lithe figure in a bear hug.

She was still laughing, her breath puffs of white in the frosty air. "You were right," she admitted, pulling back a bit to look at him. "There was a lot I needed to deal with before I was ready to become *any* man's wife. Regardless of what has happened, or will happen, I wanted to tell you that in person." A moment of hesitation seemed to cross her features with this statement.

Daniel was instantly sobered. He had just begun to realize that Grace could have simply written to him about finding peace with God—and to consider what the fact that she was *here* meant—when she emphasized that one tiny word, and gave him that look. Daniel tamped down the hope that had begun spiraling inside him. He didn't think he could stand it if she had come all this way only for closure. But cautiously he said, "Amelia told me Blake proposed, and that you were to give him an answer by Christmas."

Grace nodded. "All this fall I was planning to accept. His attentions were so soothing after my hurt." When he tried to speak, she held up a hand to stop him. "I'm ready to own my own part in what happened. Whatever you did or didn't do, it doesn't matter now, because I understand the position you were in. At least...I hope I do..." She paused, gazing up at him through thick lashes with an expression that was hopeful...and almost coy.

"Thank you, Grace, but...about Blake?" Daniel prompted. He didn't think he could endure the suspense a moment longer.

"I realized I could not marry a man I didn't love."

Daniel's breath exhaled in a whoosh.

"I told him that just before I left to come here. He was disappointed, of course, but not crushed—for I don't believe he truly loved me, either."

Trying to take this in, Daniel hung his head and closed his eyes, still lightly grasping her arms. It was just all so sudden, so unexpected, after he had spent so much time waiting and hoping.

Grace was continuing, as if oblivious to the effect her words were having on him. "Besides, now that I've had a taste of stardom, I'm not sure that being a celebrity suits me. It has its perks, but I've always suspected I was made for a more modest lifestyle. It would hardly be fair to Blake to ask him to leave the city he loves, where he works, when I'm thinking I might relocate. You see, a dear friend just told me there could be an opening for a soprano in the Christmas cantata at Tallulah's Trinity Episcopal Church. I admit I was very nervous when I got on that train. I knew I was taking a chance, coming here, but I felt this urging inside that I couldn't ignore. So…what do you think? About that opening?"

"I think," Daniel said slowly, "I hope…that God might just be giving a lonely minister his heart's desire."

"If what you say is true, a girl would need a proper invitation to stay." Grace looked steadily into his eyes. "Like redheads are apt to do, I rushed ahead once before."

"You're sure? You would be giving up the supreme accomplishment of which any singer could dream. We could consider me joining you—"

She put a finger over his lips to stop him this time. "Thank you, but I believe I've already spoken my heart on this matter, more than once." A tiny smile belied the scolding words.

Daniel captured the hand, tugged off the glove and kissed her skin. He took a deep, steadying breath. "In that case, Miss Grace Galveston, will you do me the great honor of becoming my bride?"

"I love you, Daniel Monroe, and I will."

Daniel laughed joyously, feeling like his heart might burst from the fullness. He wondered anew at God's sense of both timing and irony. Daniel could almost imagine Him laughing, too.

"I love you, Grace. But I can hardly believe this isn't a dream. There's not been a day since you left that I haven't thought of you."

"Nor I of you."

"I guess that says it all."

"Then you can finally kiss me."

Daniel bent his head and ever so slightly brushed his lips across hers, as if afraid that at his touch she might disintegrate like the falling snow. But her lips were soft and incredibly warm. She was real. This was real. He started to draw back to gaze at her just to make sure, but Grace impatiently caught his head and pressed her mouth to his. That was all the confirmation he needed. His embrace lifted her feet off the ground, and he kissed her like he'd longed to for the past six months.

When they finally parted breathlessly, Grace gasped, "Now *that* was worth the fuss I created when I left New York!"

"You came alone?" he asked incredulously.

She shrugged. "I made Maureen accompany me."

"Your aunt was livid," Daniel said with certainty.

"We'll pray for her, and she'll come around." She smirked.

"And the opera?"

"They can call up that Herbert-Forster woman whose husband plays in the orchestra."

Daniel smiled and took Grace's hand. "We once talked about how beautiful the gorge was covered in snow. Come on, my love, let me show you." He pulled her gently to the edge of the precipice and wrapped his arms around her. There they stood for a long time, looking out over Lover's Leap together.

Epilogue

And that was the beginning of my great-great-grandparents' life together.

The way I hear it told, Aunt Martha wasn't too crushed at the prospect of moving to Tallulah Falls herself, once Professor Schmidt made bold to tell her of his feelings. As she settled into life in North Georgia, the Southland settled like balm around her soul. Its soothing tones and balmy days just seemed to melt the shell she wore. And after sitting under enough of Daniel Monroe's sermons, she, too, made peace with her past and with her Lord.

When Hampton Galveston realized his daughter truly loved this Appalachian minister and was set to live her life with him, he, too, gave his blessing. He even agreed to come to the little church to give her away in a July wedding. That visit, and a growing bond with his daughter, convinced him that the mountain resort would be a perfect new vacation spot for his family.

In the years that followed, folks brought their children from miles around to be tutored by the great operatic singer, Grace Galveston Monroe. She became a legend in these parts. Many a career was launched from the Monroes' parlor. Four children and twenty-two years later, the Rev. Mrs. Monroe became a member of the faculty at the new Tallulah Falls School, oft called "The Light in the Mountains."

Yes, it's quiet here now. The grand era of tourism is over. Pine Terrace, one of the few old homes remaining, is now a restaurant. The river's dammed up. Several times a year they have what they call "aesthetic releases." I go and watch the kayakers ensconced in their bright little boats plunging over the waterfalls, which are temporarily restored to their former power and glory. Only once since the summer of 1886 has Tallulah Falls seen crowds like they did then—and that was in 1970, when another famous aerialist, Karl Wallenda, crossed the gorge on a high wire.

Yet I can imagine how it used to be. Sometimes as I sit looking out over the gorge, I think proudly of the people like my ancestors who called this land home. The legacy of music and faith Grandma Grace left to both her pupils and her descendants still lives on today. A bit of it is inside my heart.

Afterword/Acknowledgements

While the central characters in *Redeeming Grace* have been fictional, I hope their story has captured your imagination and provided a realistic glimpse of Tallulah Falls c. 1886. While Trinity Episcopal was simply a creation of this love story, the St. James Mission (Episcopal) was begun near the falls in the early 1880s. According to *Images of America: Tallulah Falls*, a church building was constructed c. 1890. The web site of beautiful Grace-Calvary Episcopal in Clarkesville provides the fascinating history of Grace Church as well as missions on the area circuit.

Some of the individuals mentioned in the story, like the Moss family, "Aunt Fannie" Smith, and Professor Leon, truly did shape Tallulah Falls in the late 1800s. I would like to thank Brian A. Boyd, communications director at Tallulah Falls School, and author of my most-used resource, *Secrets of Tallulah*, for his generous help in clarifying details about Victorian Tallulah. Special thanks also are due to Mr. John Moss for graciously providing information on his ancestors.

Many visitors enjoy the beauty of Tallulah Falls State Park every year. The Jane Hurt Yarn Interpretive Center provides wonderful information on the history, flora and fauna, and wildlife of the area. Aesthetic water releases from the dam are held each spring and fall.

This tale of romantic love and God's redeeming grace has merely skimmed the surface of all that Tallulah and Habersham County have to offer. There are more stories yet to be written.

(Note to the publisher: Other sources consulted but not mentioned above include *Habersham County, Georgia: A Pictorial History* by Jo and Stephen Whited; *Georgia Waters: Tallulah Falls, Madison Springs, Scull Shoals and the Okefenokee Swamp* by E. Merton Coulter, 1965; *The Appalachian Forest* by Chris Bolgiano, StackPole Books, 1998; *Where There Are Mountains: An Environmental History of the Southern Appalachians* by Donald Edward Davis, The University of Georgia Press, 2000; *Georgia Magazine* August 1971 article "Aunt Fannie Smith: The Famous Hostess of Sinking Mountain" by Michael Motes; Athens, Georgia, *Daily News*, Sunday, May 15, 1966 article "Family Puzzlers" by Mary Bondurant Warren; *Kobbé's Complete Opera Book* ed. & rev. by The Earl of Harewood, G. P. Putnam's Sons, NY, 1954; and numerous web sites on The Metropolitan Opera's history, Victorian-era New York City society, fashion, music, dance, the 131st New York Volunteer Infantry, historic Darien, Georgia, and historic Habersham County, Georgia.)

Printed in the United States
45619LVS00002B/28-129

9 781424 115099